Climbing Veritas Mountain

One Man's Journey with the Lord

Ryan Paul Young

iUniverse, Inc.
New York   Bloomington

iUniverse books may be ordered through booksellers or by contacting:

iUniverse
1663 Liberty Drive
Bloomington, IN 47403
www.iuniverse.com
1-800-Authors (1-800-288-4677)

ISBN: 978-1-4502-1942-6 (sc)
ISBN: 978-1-4502-1944-0 (dj)
ISBN: 978-1-4502-1943-3 (ebook)

Printed in the United States of America

iUniverse rev. date: 03/19/2010

CONTENTS

This Book is dedicated:

- To my parents for forming me in the Truth.
- To my wife for keeping me in the Truth.
- To my children: What is provided in this book is the most important message I can give you as your father: I love you all. I will see you at the finish line….

Epigraph

Jesus says in John 8:32,

"...the **truth** will set you free."

Veritas

The word **Veritas** is the Latin word for **Truth**.

What is Truth?
1. That which is considered to be the Supreme Reality and to have the ultimate meaning and value of existence.
2. Conformity to Reality.

Forward

It is with tremendous honor that I take the opportunity to comment on the content of this book and the amazing man behind its words. Having known Ryan since the tender age of 18, I have had the pleasure of being by his side throughout his evolution into the man of God he is today. He is, among other things, a loving and steadfast husband, father and son, an evangelist, and a seeker of Truth and justice. He has conquered many obstacles to become those things over the years and has been a hero to me with his unwavering devotion to discerning the will of God in his life.

If there is one impression many people have after a conversation with Ryan, it is that he is passionate and dedicated to not only what he currently believes, but also to the search for something more: Truth. I have witnessed him spending his adult life in the pursuit of wisdom and justice, attempting to learn more about the God with whom he wants to spend the rest of his eternal life. His spiritual journey has consisted mainly of seeking, recognizing, internalizing, defending, teaching, and sharing little morsels of truth he has gathered throughout the years.

Collecting the tidbits set forth in this book about various subjects has been an adventure of sorts. Ryan would not consider himself a scholar, but he has been open to hearing and absorbing the advice and insights of all of those around him, likeminded or not. I have been with my husband for the formation of many of the thoughts in this book, whether derived from meditation, dinners with friends and family, consults with his patients, books, the Bible, the Catholic Catechism, or even movies. I can attest to the earnest process by which Ryan carefully and prayerfully separates out the truth in what he hears and reads. This book was not meant to be a textbook, but Ryan has painstakingly tried to ascertain the validity of his opinions prior to including them. If there are items that do not conform to the truths held within Catholic teaching, I can assure you that it is truly unintentional on his part.

Along the way, many of our friends and relatives have been instrumental in not only shaping and refining Ryan's thoughts, but also encouraging the propagation of these teachings through inviting him to speak to a large group or supporting him in the formation of a youth camp. Ryan has formed stores of appropriate stories and words of wisdom for various daily struggles and has been bold enough to share these when he encountered someone in need of comfort or help finding God. Thus began the process many, many years ago of starting to record the stories mainly so he would not forget them. This book has now evolved into a record of these insights; however, it began as simply a way for a loving father to share his journey with the Lord for the sake of his children. As a father, he wants only that his children have eternal life with God. His secondary desire is for his children to know him, love him and want to be with him forever, much as Ryan's only life's goal has become to know God, love God, and be with Him forever in Heaven.

Ryan firmly believes that we are in a war for souls. In writing this book, he hopes to arm his children with a shield of self-awareness and a sword of Truth. I could not be more proud of the man Ryan has become, and in many ways has always been. He is a true inspiration to me, our family, our friends and our community and I am not ashamed to say that I consider myself the luckiest woman alive to be at his side in his journey to Christ. Enjoy this book as I have enjoyed immensely the many nights we have labored together over the formation of its contents.

Forever in Christ,

Elizabeth Young

Prologue

I am not an author. I am not even a decent writer. I have never in my wildest imagination ever contemplated that I would be sitting down at this moment, writing to you. I have no real expectation that a single soul will ever read this book. I am not in control.

I am on a journey. This journey is a walk with the Lord where my only task is to let Him lead the way. This journey has thus far taken me in directions I didn't know were possible for me. He has requested of me things I did not think I could do. I have no knowledge of where the Lord will take me in this life. I am not in control.

This conversation with you is the next step in my walk with the Lord. For some reason, the Lord has requested me to write down little bits of wisdom I have learned so far in my short life. I don't fully understand the Lord's reasoning in this venture. After all, I am a very weak man, sinful in thought and deed. The only power I have is to choose to obey God or not. I am not in control.

Throughout my whole life I have wanted to be in control. I wanted to know and to ensure that I would be "successful" in everything I did. I found that I had a skewed worldly perception of "success." I measured success in dollars, influence, power, praise, and control of others. I formerly would have questioned myself at this moment, asking "why am I taking the time to write a book that I do not know a soul on this earth will actually publish, much less read?" I asked myself this before giving up my time because I didn't want to give up control over my time. A constant struggle within me is restraining *my* will to control. I must repeatedly shut down my instinct to control, rooted in Original Sin, and try to live a life where I am not in control.

If I can give up my control, I can truly be free from failure and worry because in a spiritual sense, there is **no such thing as failure in** *attempting* **to do the will of the Lord.** The Lord does not guarantee "success" as I would have formerly defined it. I believe He does guarantee peace and joy and ultimately eternal salvation for those who allow Him to control the path of their life. The reality is that worldly success no longer matters as much to me because in attempting to do the will of the Lord, I feel I have already eternally succeeded.

Again, I do not fully understand why the Lord has requested that I write down some of the Truth He has shared with me. I am not even fully clear about how I learned much of what I will share with you. I do know that if you are reading this book, **it is not by accident**. Hopefully one of the lessons the Lord has taught me in my life may be applicable to you.

I pray at this moment that I have the courage to write what the Lord intends. I pray that those reading this can dive into the arms of the Lord as would a child, finding peace, joy, and eternal bliss. I pray that I never forget that I am not in control....

Ryan Paul Young

THE MEANING
OF LIFE

TICK TOCK, TICK TOCK, tick tock... time. I started to think a lot about time when I was just beginning high school. Time was passing and passing by quickly and I didn't have a point to my life. I found myself locked in a routine. We all know about routines. Mine consisted of waking up before sunrise to the obnoxious beeping of my alarm clock, showering in cold water (I was always competing for hot water with my six sisters), eating nearly the same thing every day for breakfast and lunch, waiting for the bus, going to class, working after school, watching TV, talking to friends and then repeating the same pointless routine, day after day after day. I never enjoyed doing anything in my life unless I had a reason and at that time, without a purpose, I ultimately didn't enjoy doing much at all. At the end of my days I knew I was going to die. Whether I liked it or not, this was a hard, cold fact. Why bother with the effort of life if it would all end anyway? Without a reason to my life, I was living a life without peace and joy. I felt empty.

Before having purpose and meaning to my life, I had moments of "happiness." These moments would even be experienced during times of sin. I would feel happy when I felt "full" emotionally, physically, and mentally. The problem with my life and my actions at that time was that the happiness that I experienced was fleeting and brief. I was always looking for the next big fix, which might be experienced with one more vacation, one more material good, one more girlfriend, one more achieved earthly success. I was never able to sustain that feeling of "happiness" and would always return to that inner void of emptiness. What I really sought was meaning and purpose to my life.

I call it the "Superbowl Syndrome." Imagine a professional athlete practicing football his whole life and finally making the NFL. After years in the NFL, he finally makes it on a team that wins a lot of games. He gives it his all throughout the season, diving and fighting for the ball. He finally makes it to the Superbowl and his team wins. He experiences absolute jubilation and 'happiness' for about five minutes. He then asks himself, "now what?" I had to reevaluate. What were my 'Superbowl' ambitions? Were my objectives *lasting* objectives?

Since then I have observed thousands of people, of all ages, wandering through life the way I did in high school. I used to work in New York City and commute every day on the train. People in suits would be holding the same kind of coffee in one hand, with the same newspaper in the other, and would know the exact spot where the train door would open once it would finally arrive. They would enter the train and sit in the same seat they always used, turn to their left and say, "Good morning Fred," then to their right and say, "Good morning Susie." It is not that I perceived routine as evil. Rather it is routine without purpose and meaning that kills our spiritual being. It was like a "rat race" where the rat wasn't even really in a race but was running on a treadmill and going nowhere. It was on this commute that I thought about how far the Lord had taken me up to that point in time. I realized with joy that I had been spared becoming a machine. In finding purpose, I jumped off of the conveyer belt of pointless routine. I had been spared spiritual death.

I was able to avoid that fate because I stopped to ask the question: Why? Why are we here? What is the point of life? I believe all humans have asked these questions consciously or subconsciously at some time during their life. I believe we are all built with a consuming hunger for the Truth.

The first question I think we must all address is as follows: Is there is a God? If I saw a piece of trash, such as a cardboard box, lying on the sidewalk, would I think that the box existed by mere chance? Would I truly believe that different organic material such as trees spontaneously broke down into an evolutionary cycle of organic soup and through millions of years formed itself into a cardboard box? Or would I just think to myself, "WHO put the cardboard box in the middle of the sidewalk?" As simple as a box is, I would logically assume that someone made and designed that box. Similarly, I can't look at a human being without awe knowing the complexity of our design. Logically, there has to be a designer. After all, am I not more complicated than a cardboard box?

Thinking of it a different way; is it realistic to imagine a tornado blowing through a junkyard and, through chance alone, creating a 747 airliner with all of the working circuit boards and capacity to fly? I don't look at an airplane and think to myself, "Boy, the Big Bang really did a terrific job in creating that aircraft." Logically, I would have some faith that this 747 must be the design of some engineer. I would marvel at the engineer that could create such an amazing thing. Am I not more complex than a 747 airplane?

Human beings are not only built with created matter which allows us to function and move, but we have also been built with life. We have the capacity to think, love, communicate, dream, laugh, cry, empathize, hope, forgive, create, and feel. You can't get these abilities in a rock or atom or molecule independently. There must be a creator.

The fact that we were designed so well is amazing but our *maintained* existence is also a miracle in and of itself. In my professional life, I work in the field of medicine. It is surprising to see how easy it is to die. It is incredible how many parts have to work perfectly for us to be able to live. If one organ system is not perfect, we die. The fact that our heart beats without our effort 60-100 beats per minute and if it stops for several minutes we die, *that* is a miracle. The fact that we go through our entire lives able to breathe air and if we were to stop breathing for several minutes we die, *that* is a miracle. Our body's capacity to repair cells automatically when we heal is a miracle. Knowing what I know about the human body and about what can go wrong with our bodies, I can't believe we can actually live to be 100 years of age.

The whole notion that we can exist without God, our designer and engineer, is rather absurd to me. It simply does not follow basic rules of "science." One such scientific rule is that something cannot come from nothing. Even with the argument that the matter in the "Big Bang" could have existed forever (which I don't believe), it still does not explain how the matter of the universe spontaneously and accidentally could create life, let alone create a life form that possesses the ability to think and love.

Professionally, I am also a scientist of sorts. I think the world mistakenly perceives that science is the attempt to disprove the existence of God. I believe that **science is the study of the creation of God.** As I look at science in that light, it completely enhances my knowledge of God and Creation and consequently, my relationship with God deepens even further. I am able to marvel at His grandeur in space, the environment, and our bodies.

I am not alone in this view of science. Many scientists initially set out to disprove God and then discovered in their scientific pursuit that the mathematical possibility of us existing without Him is essentially impossible. I would argue that it would require far more "faith" to be an atheist than to be someone who acknowledges the existence of God.

What about evolution? I don't think it matters. Evolution does not disprove God. You would still need God to create something before that something could evolve. You would still need order and oversight to keep life in existence. If God created the universe and that universe evolved with God's oversight, who cares whether or not evolution exists? The Truth is He created us either way.

In my experience, I have found that God has made man "in His image and likeness."(Gen1:26) There are many aspects of this belief, but one part of that likeness is our ability to create. Keep in mind that man cannot create independently. We cannot make something from nothing. We can only change creation's form. For example, we can create a pottery bowl from clay; we cannot create the clay itself from nothing. In essence, God allows us to co-create with Him and, in doing so, we can hopefully understand Him better.

After we conclude that God must exist, I still questioned, "why me?" Why did He create me? Why give us this life? In my observation of people, I came to a startling realization: we have been *given* everything that identifies us. We were born into our bodies, our looks, talents, family, country, wealth, station, everything. We had no control over any of these things at birth. We have limited control over these realities even as we get older. Whether you were born predisposed to being rich, poor, fat, skinny, ugly, gorgeous, psychologically imbalanced, stupid, intelligent, or any combination thereof, we all have only one thing in common from birth: **our free will.** The only common attribute of all human beings is the ability to choose, moment to moment, what we are going to do with the station, talents, looks, intelligence, wealth, and so forth that we have been given. This Truth brought me to understand the meaning of life. **THE MEANING OF LIFE IS TO CHOOSE GOD!!!!**

We have been given this split second, this blink of eternity's eye, to make a choice. Again, I found that if I believe in God and understand that my only possession is my free will, what else could this life be for? Think about it for a minute; if you loved someone, would you force them to be with you for eternity? Can there be love without freedom to choose it? If God were to create us without choice and chain us to Heaven's wall, could you call that love or would it become slavery?

In order for us to have the capacity to love, we must have the choice of not loving. Love itself cannot exist without a free-will. Once I understood that my purpose in life is this decision to choose Him, to choose Love, everything came into focus. Now there is a reason for my existence. Now there is a purpose to every breath I take on a daily basis. Now there is a reason for every action and decision I make. Life has become a lot more fun.

Once I found that Heaven is my objective, my entire "priority list of life" changed. My relationship with God and His mission for me now takes precedence over all my former "worldly" goals. The truth is that if I am the most "successful" individual in every earthly way, including family, money, power, education, and earthly influence, and if I die and have not chosen God, my entire life has been an utter waste.

Now, the priority of my life is to strive for eternity with God. That priority influences every decision I make. This influenced which college I attended, who I decided to marry, what major I chose in college, my political affiliation… everything. There is no decision on earth that would warrant ignoring the objective of Heaven and choosing God.

This concept of striving to make eternity with God the priority of my life has changed my entire decision making process. For example, these principles even applied to picking my children's school. Heaven is clearly the priority of the school we chose. The children are very innocent and hopefully maintain that childlike innocence through the eighth grade. Let's imagine that the academic education was not stellar and there were more challenging academic options. Ultimately, I would have an internal debate about what is more important, my child's mind or their soul. I would then come to the ultimate question, "If my children were the smartest people in Hell, have I done my job as their father?"

In understanding the meaning of life, I now experience joy. The difference between happiness and joy is that joy lasts. I perpetually feel good at my emotional baseline. I feel other emotions like sadness, anger, jealousy, happiness, ambition, inadequacy, and so forth, but at my baseline, I always return to joy. I have peace. I know where I came from and where I am going. The journey of life has become easier and now I feel like I am moving downhill.

Not everyone in the world has *worldly* freedom. Some people are born into tyranny. However, with a free will, we can all have *spiritual* freedom. We have the freedom to use our free will in every situation, good or bad, and we have the freedom to use our free will to choose God… or not.

Please don't think I am saying that if you understand the meaning of your life, you will not suffer. The truth is quite different. The truth is that even while suffering—if you and I understand that in every moment of every day we have an opportunity to choose God—we can be joyful in that suffering. This was shown by the first Christian martyrs as they were burned alive or fed to lions in the Coliseum. They were joyful and singing at their deaths. That joy and exuberance caused many observers to convert to Christianity. Another example is that of Saint Maximilian Kolbe. He was incarcerated in a concentration camp during World War II. He tried at every moment, good and bad, to choose God. He maintained such a level of joy and holiness that many, including his cell mates, were converted to Christianity through their recognition of his joy. The point is this: **if you constantly choose God, you will have peace and joy at all times, in every situation**. It was when I realized the meaning of my life that my adventure with the Lord began.

CHOICE

It is 8:23AM in Baghdad Iraq. This day, my mission and the fulfillment and culmination of my life will reach its apex. Thirteen minutes left. I am excited and anxious at this moment. I can feel the sweat of my body covering my forehead under my turban and running down my back. I don't know if I am sweating because of the stifling heat? I don't know if it's from the weight of my deliverance buckled around my waist? I don't know if it's from fear? I am so petrified that I can taste bile in my mouth. Regardless, the harem that awaits me in heaven as promised by my earthly spiritual guide, Mohammed Al Jahiff, is worth a bit of sweat and fear. I finally received the call by cell phone last night. I have prepared my whole life for this moment at my madrasa and I will not fail. These American infidels and Iraqi traitors of Islam are about to be defeated. I feel honored that I can play a role in this holy Jihad. Here comes my target. These guys have no idea about what is about to hit them. It is time to reach for the trigger. Three, two, one, Praise ALLAH!..... BOOM!

This teenage Islamic male just died believing he was choosing God. Was he? How do we know? What is our standard for that perfect choice? Many will read that story and start a mental series of justifications for why they don't believe in "organized religion." They convince themselves to suspend the search for Truth altogether, and continue going out of their way to avoid God as much as possible. They will choose to live life without meaning or purpose, choosing a finite life of emptiness and ignorance and will ignore the bigger picture.

This is frequently acted out with a public display of false spiritual humility with statements like, "How can I even begin to try to know or understand anything about something as great as God"... trying to be "humble" through ignorance and avoidance of reason. In reality, most of these "intellectuals" are just spiritually lazy.

What is ironic about this is that these same intellectuals generally argue that they believe in the concept of good and evil. They generally agree that the concepts of the Ten Commandments and charity and so forth are "good acts." This basic understanding of good and evil is also called "Natural Law." Natural Law is an imprint God has placed on the heart of every human being to help identify the basics of good versus evil. If one believes in good and evil, inherently they must also believe in God because otherwise "good" would not be defined by anything and there would be chaos. **Without God, there is no order. Without God, there is no Truth. Without God, there is no such thing as good and evil.**

I do not believe God would create us and give us a free will to then abandon us to live lives without purpose or meaning. God gave us the perfect standard. He gave us "the Way, the Truth, and the Life."(Jn 14:16) He gave us *Himself* as Jesus Christ. You could not find an example more perfect than God himself. No longer is the choice for God ambiguous. No longer is Truth some vague, abstract, unattainable idea.

Why Jesus? Why not Mohammed, or John Smith, or Buddha and so forth? I ultimately had to ask myself this question, "If I were to choose from all the prophets and holy men throughout time to be my savior, my 'perfect choice,' who would it be?" If the meaning of life is to choose God, I have yet to find another religion where God Himself came to Earth to be the "Perfect Choice" and ultimately redeem mankind. Other religions have a "great prophet," but they don't claim to have God Himself.

The basic moral standard of our country and most the world is generally, "love your brother as yourself." The world's basic moral standard (Natural Law) follows the teaching of Jesus, whether the world knows this or not. There is no individual throughout all of time that more dramatically changed the world's view of morality than Jesus Christ. If you are reading this book and do not know about the life of Jesus Christ, I implore you to read the Gospels in the New Testament or even watch the movie "Jesus of Nazareth,"(1977) a wonderful, scripturally based movie about the life of Jesus. Once you do that, you will then have to make a decision identified accurately by C.S. Lewis in "Mere Christianity." That decision is as follows: either Jesus is a complete lunatic because He claims to be the Son of Man (God Himself), or Jesus Christ is who He claims He is. How could He be considered a "great prophet" or "nice historical figure" if He was a lunatic and a liar? Which do you believe?

If you have a general knowledge of the life of Christ, and you are not sure whether He is a lunatic and a liar, or that Christ is truly the Son of God, I ask you to consider performing a simple spiritual exercise. Find a large crucifix. Stare at Jesus on the cross and repeat aloud ten times the following: Jesus, You are a lunatic, a liar, and a fraud; You did not die on that cross for me. Performing this exercise may help you get "off the fence" and make a decision. If you can make it through that statement ten times and mean it, the rest of this book will not be very relevant to you.

Evidence of Christ's divinity was demonstrated by the stories documented throughout the New Testament. This was seen through His miracles that were acknowledged by both His friends and His enemies. It was seen at His birth when Herod was willing to kill all male children less than two years of age in Christ's hometown to prevent Christ from maturing. It was seen by Three Kings coming to pay Him homage. This was proven as He rose from the dead. Christ's message fulfills the longing for Truth in every human heart. Christ's divinity is confirmed in that all of His apostles except John were tortured to death and martyred for their faith. Were they willing to die for a hoax or a lie?

If you are with me up to this point and believe that God created us, gave us a free will to choose Him, and that Jesus is the Truth, the perfect choice, then welcome to Christianity! Accepting the Bible as an authority for Truth only then makes sense. The entire Old Testament points to the coming of the Messiah. It is incredible that the lessons of the Old Testament and spiritual struggles of mankind thousands of years before the birth of Christ are the same battles we fight today. The Truth in Scripture stands out for this reason. Its Truth transcends time. The entire Old Testament ultimately provides only a shadow of God and His will for us. Through the Old Testament God communicates through signs and wonders and prophets. It is only in the New Testament where the shadow of God is lifted by God Himself by becoming directly present to His people in the person of Christ Jesus. God has made it clear that if we can emulate Christ and follow His teaching, we will make the "perfect choice."

Christ was Jewish and accepted the laws of the Old Testament for Himself. This validates the Truths set forth in the Old Testament. I don't believe the Son of God would follow the Old Testament unless the principles were true. The New Testament describes Christ Himself through the Gospels and the Apostles' accounts of their direct witness of Him. Again, logically, if Christ is the Messiah, the New Testament can be considered as True and inspired by God. It would not make sense for the God of the universe to become man to reveal to us the "Way, Truth and Life" only to die for our sins and not leave us any Truth of His teaching for mankind. It is therefore logical to believe that if Christ is the Messiah and the accounts of His life were inspired by God, the New Testament is also a valid "authority" in Truth.

If Christ is the Way, the Truth, and the Life, there is no further prophet needed to relay the wishes of God. Who can better offer us Truth than God Himself? That is why other religious texts, such as the Koran or the Book of Mormon, are not necessary in the search for Truth. Christ didn't say "I am *mostly* the Truth and some other prophet will need to come after my time and finish the job…" As far as I know, neither Islam nor Mormons believe that Christ is a lunatic or a liar. The reasoning for the need of the teaching of Mohammed or John Smith is therefore unclear to me. That being said, many Muslims and Mormons, through their inherent desire to be good and follow "Natural Law," *live* the life of Christ better than some Christians. Who then, is making a better "choice" for God?

In my walk with the Lord, the awareness of these realities started to bring focus to my divine mission. That mission is to know Christ and to follow Christ. Little did I know then that, in doing so, the Truth would set me free. In following Christ, I am free from the mental and spiritual programming of our society and culture. I am no longer deceived with the lie that money, power, and sex will bring me lasting joy. In many ways, by following Christ, I have experienced a taste of Heaven here on Earth. By acknowledging the Truth of Christ, I now have a spiritual focus and can live in the Truth with the confidence of knowing right from wrong, good from evil. I can be confident about the impact of my behavior. I now have a goal of perfection that I can attempt to reach. I now have peace and joy. Jesus truly is the Way, the Truth, and the Life!

THE RELIGION OF
INDIVIDUALISM

I RECENTLY ATTENDED A MASS in upstate New York, and noted that the church was sparsely populated. Those who were in attendance were old. The priest himself was old. In fact, the priest is the pastor for several parishes. There is only one shared Mass per weekend. Other than my family, there was no one in attendance under the age of 60. There was not even an organist. The church is terminally ill in this region. It will likely not exist ten years from now. I have attended many churches throughout the Northeast and noticed similar situations. The Catholic Church, as we know it, is dying in that area of our country.

It reminds me of my college semester abroad in Europe. I went into these fantastic, immense cathedrals throughout France, Germany, Hungary, and the Czech Republic only to find the cathedrals nearly empty for Mass. It was like walking into a cold, dark tomb. These massive buildings were corpses of the life that once lived within them. That life was the Church, the community of believers who once worshipped together in unison as one body. The members of this community cared for one another and were connected to the lives of the other members. This community shared in each family's high points, such as a baptism and first communion, and would also be there for a family's low points, such as providing help when needed or being present to lend support during the death of one of its members. The church was a spiritual family then.

One afternoon I was talking to one of my childhood best friends. We were reflecting on the condition of the Catholic Church in today's society. I was very sad at the prospect of such goodness in our Church seemingly dying in my sight. He said something very profound. He noted that we now live in a society of individualism where the very concept of community and family is under full attack. With the family community under attack, the attack on the larger church community of the faithful would reasonably follow. In short, **the Church is ill because the family is ill.**

This made a lot of sense to me. We now live in the age of "Seinfeld." I love watching that show. I still capture the episodes on my DVR. I find the program quite humorous. However, what disturbs me is that many of my friends and peers are actually living lives like those portrayed on that show. On the program you see four people living individual lives without a serious commitment to anything or anybody. They are gods unto themselves. There is never a moment when any one of them would sacrifice anything for anybody else. They simply live an amoral life, finding the next "fix" of happiness with their next meal, date, or entertainment prospect. Every moment of every day their goal is to satisfy every animalistic desire… to feel emotionally full for a few moments. This drive to satisfy their emotional hunger is at any cost, regardless of the damage done to themselves, others, or the community at large. In the end there is nothing but absolute emptiness and loneliness. Instead of watching this TV series as an entertaining fictional story and satire of our culture, the "Seinfeld lifestyle" has now become the cultural "norm."

When I decided to ask my wife to marry me, I cannot tell you how many people told me to wait until I "established myself" before I got married. In essence, I was told to live the religion of individualism before giving myself up to the commitment of family. In the religion of individualism, *my* needs were to come first. If it feels good, do it. In the religion of individualism, *I* am in control. In this religion, *I* am god. *My* education was to come first. *My* job and income and career were to come first. There was nothing more important than *my* immediate pleasure and *my* quest for power. If I was lonely on my quest for power, I could always live with a woman and pretend we were married without any commitment. If we were to get pregnant, we could always abort. After all, *my* needs were to always come first. I have been programmed by society to believe that marriage might be a threat to the control I wanted in my life. After all, *I* was programmed that *I* was god.

When you stop to think about it, our entire culture is presently driven by control which people equate to power. How many people do you know that want to control when, where, and how many children they will allow to enter their life? Most are only thinking about how much power they will lose in their careers if they do not control this. Instead of seeing children as immense gifts of God, children are viewed as burdens and as a threat to the religion of individualism, or as a prize to be manufactured when we want.

How many divorces have you heard about where one spouse is considered no longer convenient and, through infidelity by the other spouse, is therefore tossed aside like yesterday's garbage, all for the struggle for personal esteem and power? How many of us put our careers first instead of our family? How many people unnecessarily work too many hours away from home for their personal glory and not for the glory of God or for the direct benefit of their family? How many of us use our power over our time to spend more hours watching television than to spend time with our children? I was one of those people. In many ways, I still am. I fight against this "original sin" every moment of every day. I am weak.

Our latest government "stimulus bill" is one more symptom of this "religion of individualism." We used to live in a country where we worked hard in order to provide our children with a future better than our own. We now "borrow" money from our children to get every entitlement we can drown ourselves in today. We are selfish.

Through our desire to control everything and be gods, the family unit and the essence of community are under attack. The family is like an orchestra with many parts that, when working in unison, creates a symphony. If everyone in the family is playing their own tune, the resulting music will sound disastrous. The family is the building block of all society. If society does not have a solid base in the family, all aspects of that society will suffer and ultimately collapse. Think about how many problems are rampant in our society today due to the lack of a strong family unit. Think about how many families no longer have a matriarch and a patriarch. The fight for control and power in our lives are causing divorce and fornication and selfishness to become our cultural "norm." In this modern era, are we truly better off? Do more people have lasting joy in their lives?

The Church is a family. The Church is a community. The Church is referred to as "The body of Christ."(1Cor12:12) **The Church is the antithesis of the religion of individualism.**

In the "church" of my home, my family helps keep me grounded. I am married to my Elizabeth. We gave ourselves to each other, totally and completely, in the holy sacrament of Matrimony. Throughout the natural development of our marital relationship over the past eleven years, I have truly come to understand the statement that "two come together and make one flesh."(Mt 19:5) She is me. I am her. We are inseparable. We are at the level of union where she can read me and my mind without verbal communication. She knows without my input when something is on my mind. She knows when I am sad or angry. It is somewhat unbelievable how well she truly knows everything about me. The greatest aspect of our relationship is that, in fully giving of ourselves to each other, we experience unconditional love. With that level of love, I have no fear. I am free knowing that as long as I draw breath, she will be committed to me and I her. There is nothing I can do or she could do that would jeopardize that reality. This allows complete honesty in our relationship. When I battle the demons in my life, especially with the religion of individualism, she draws me back, she draws me home. She reminds me about the meaning to my life. She reminds me about our community at home and about my responsibility within that "body." She reminds me about my priorities in the big picture. My soul is hers to tend to. In my commitment to her and to my family, I am fulfilling my vocation. I am doing what God intends for me to do. I have reason and purpose in my life. By fulfilling my commitment to my family, my church community, and my God, I am at peace.

Our family community is a microcosm of the larger family, our Church. Ideally, we *could* give of ourselves, totally and completely to each other, experiencing unconditional love with everybody, all the time. In doing this, we would truly be making the "perfect choice" as set forth by Christ. In giving up the religion of individualism, in giving up our control, we become truly free. True community *can be* experienced. The church in our region would then thrive as its members would experience peace and joy. Again, this possibility can happen only if the family cell is repaired and healed. How can we repair the community of the Church if our "church" at home is in disrepair?

By identifying the enemy as the religion of individualism, we now can take active steps in avoiding its downfall. Become aware of how we are being programmed through our public education and media. Resist becoming the "army of one." Give up control to God and become "like a child."(Lk18:17) Make an active choice of your will to first lead your family in becoming a community. Spend time with your spouse and children. Eat meals with them. Talk, think, sing, play, and simply *be* with them. Then take your family and participate in the family of your religious faith and then the greater community at large. Make a difference. In starting this mission, I asked myself what kind of difference my family could realistically make. The reality is that Christ started out with just twelve apostles. There are now over a billion Christians in the world. **With the Holy Spirit, there is no such thing as odds.**

THERE IS A GOD
AND I AM NOT HIM

ONE NIGHT AS I was mentally preparing for a Confirmation class I was to teach several days later, I asked the Lord in prayer if He had any ideas. He responded that evening as I was falling asleep. I was reminded of a scene in a movie called "Rudy" (1993) that I saw ten years earlier. The movie was about a college student who was desperately trying to transfer into Notre Dame University. During his third and final attempt he was praying in the cathedral. An elderly priest sat down to talk to him and Rudy asked the priest if there was anything else he could do to get into Notre Dame. The priest replied, "In all my years as a Catholic priest, I have come to two significant conclusions. First, there is a God. Second, I am not Him."

When I first saw the movie, that line didn't register at all. I do not believe the writer of that movie knew how radically profound that statement is when he was making the film. When thinking about the class I was about to teach, and thinking more deeply about that statement from the movie, I concluded that the statement **"There is a God and I am not Him"** is the most important lesson of my life. If you absorb nothing else from this book other than "There is a God and I am not Him," you will be in pretty good spiritual shape.

Looking at that lesson superficially, I thought "Of course I am not God." Then I started evaluating *my* life, *my* priorities, *my* behavior, and *my* beliefs and found that, in many ways, I actually try to *be God* unto myself all the time.

I found I want control of everything. I want to control my time, my environment, my belongings, the people around me, my money, my children, my wife, my job. Especially with regard to sin, I wanted to define the Truth for myself. If I fell short of the "bar of perfection" established by Christ, I would set the bar lower for my convenience. After all, we have all heard from our culture "what is true for you is true for you and what is true for me is true for me." I didn't realize at the time that what that statement really says is that there is *no* Truth, we are all just making it up as we go along. Therefore, with this flawed line of thinking, ultimately the Truth is *relative*. If I am a god unto myself, and you are a god unto yourself, then who is right? Where does the Truth lie? If the principle is that everybody's truth is right, is there such a thing as Truth? In reality, mankind has always searched for Truth. When Pontius Pilate was interrogating Christ, even he asked, "What is Truth?"

I am Roman Catholic. I find many within our Faith saying "I am a Catholic but I don't believe in...." These issues include the Church's teaching on fornication, abortion, divorce, contraception, woman becoming priests, and so forth. Some want a buffet of alternative truths. I want some of this and not some of that. In essence, what I was doing in my youth was making up my own religion, called "Ryanism," whereby I made up truths as I saw fit. What I failed to ask myself was this: if I believe the Church is true in most areas, how did the Church lose its authority in the Truth in areas in which I disagreed?

Many of us live by the standards of behavior we set for ourselves. We make up our own code of morality and we make up our own rules. **If we believe that morality and Truth are relative and individual, we cannot believe in God.** God defines perfection in all areas. He is Perfect Love, Mercy, Power, Justice, Knowledge, and ultimately Reality. **If you really believe in God, you therefore must believe in objective Truth.**

In discovering that "there is a God and I am not Him," I began to understand that there is *objective, unadulterated* Truth: Truth that is still true whether I like it or not; Truth that is still true whether or not I have a different opinion; Truth that is still true whether or not I have the ability to live up to that standard. Truth is not a democracy. Truth is not an opinion poll. Truth is *reality*. I have a free will to accept it… or reject it and practice Ryanism. If "there is a God and I am not Him," then there is Truth that transcends the desires of my will and what I prefer to make up on my own.

I am not the first person to have a struggle with this basic principle. We have been trying to be God unto ourselves since the beginning of mankind as described in the Bible, Genesis chapter 3: 1-5

"Now the serpent was the most cunning of all the animals that the Lord God had made. The serpent asked the woman, "Did God really tell you not to eat from any of the trees in the garden?" The woman answered the serpent: "We may eat of the fruit of the trees in the garden; it is only about the fruit of the tree in the middle of the garden that God said, 'You shall not eat it or even touch it, lest you die.' But the serpent said to the woman: "You certainly will not die! No, God knows well that the moment you eat of it your eyes will be opened and you will BE LIKE GODS WHO WILL KNOW WHAT IS GOOD AND WHAT IS BAD."

Sound familiar? Is this not the same situation we face every day of our lives? The first sin was not merely a sin of disobedience. More significantly, it was the *original sin* whereby Mankind first decided to be "like God." I too, have tasted that apple. I grab that apple with two hands and take a big juicy bite out of it every time I desire to be God unto myself. The deadly spiritual principle of *moral relativism*, the failure to accept the objective Truth of God, entered the world that instant.

Trying to *be God* has been the root of all evil on this planet from the very beginning of civilized man. Genesis was written at least two thousand years prior to the birth of Christ and it was traditionally thought to have been referring to a time four thousand years before Christ. As I said earlier, the principles of Scripture transcend time. The principles of Scripture continue to speak to the heart of mankind today. If the principles of Scripture are true, and God is Truth, then in the depth of our soul we can recognize Truth and still learn from Scripture today. Our hearts long to be filled by God, who is Truth.

As a consequence of Man's disobedience to God, and, more importantly, the attempt to be God unto ourselves, death entered the world. As I was growing up, I thought of this as only physical death. I have since learned that it is far deeper than that. When we try to be God, we welcome *spiritual* death into our lives. *Every sin* is rooted in this desire to be God. Sin is ultimately the spiritual sickness that can cause death to our souls.

Here is the good news. In His mercy, justice, and love, God also gives mankind the path out of physical and spiritual death. In the same chapter in Genesis He says to the serpent, "I will put enmity between you and the woman, and between your offspring and hers; He will strike at your head, while you strike at His heel."

God is already laying out a plan for our salvation in the same chapter of Genesis. He is already telling us about the reality of His only beloved son, His Word, His Truth, entering the world to defeat physical and spiritual death and satisfy divine, eternal justice.

Cardinal Ratzinger, in his last homily prior to becoming Pope Benedict XVI, said "No longer can we live in a world of moral relativism. We have Truth and His name is Jesus Christ!" I heard that line and felt instantly that God would choose him to become our next pope.

Through the fall of our first parents, Adam and Eve, we have all inherited the desire to *be God* in our own lives. I struggle with this on a daily basis. We call that struggle "original sin." If you think this doesn't apply to you, ask yourself this question: The last time I prayed, what did the prayer sound like? I used to pray "God, heal this person. God, help me get a raise at my job. God, let me get an A on my test. God, make this person leave me alone. God, put an end to my suffering." In these scenarios, who is God? If I was trying to be a god even in my prayer life, how many other places in my life was I failing to allow God to be in control?

In my prayer life, like most of the rest of my life, I wanted to control God. If He didn't jump as high as I requested, I would penalize our relationship with doubt. It was like being in a baseball game and I was the coach telling God (the player) what to do. I have since changed how I pray. If one of my children asks me for junk food all day long, I say "no" to prevent them from getting a stomachache. If the same child asks for a piece of fruit, the answer is always "yes." **God will**

always answer your prayer if it is healthy for you. I have learned to pray for attributes that will strengthen my soul to allow me to be a better disciple of the Lord and hopefully allow me to enter Heaven for eternity. In receiving these attributes, one can have a glimpse of Heaven *now* with daily, lasting joy. My prayers now consist of asking God to give me strength and courage to do His will. This includes requests for inner peace, patience, fortitude, and humility. In praying for others, I pray that they develop a better relationship with the Lord. I pray to more fully understand the Truth. I pray for wisdom in guiding my family. I have learned to also repent and evaluate my life and my actions. Finally, I simply use prayer to praise God and thank Him for everything. One caution: I have learned to be careful about what I ask for in prayer. I have discovered that most of the virtues and attributes I want come at a cost: *suffering.* Fortitude, patience, humility, wisdom, and so forth are frequently acquired by one making mistakes and then humbly learning from them.

In preparing for a talk I was going to give to teenagers recently, a thought I received in prayer was that I had to *"die to myself."* If my free will is the only thing that is truly my own, what that really means is that I *must die to my will.* I then thought of a scene from the mini-series "Band of Brothers" (2001). The setting was a battlefield in World War II. One soldier was a hero, running in the open, taking enemy fire at every turn to complete his mission. A second soldier was cowering in a ditch, completely paralyzed in fear. The soldier in the ditch finally asked the hero how he had the courage to run through the battlefield. The hero answered, **"Because I am already dead."**

If we could die to ourselves, if we could die to our will, we would lose all of our fear and become "born again" (Jn 3:3) as children in Christ. If our will could simply and only be to serve the Lord at every moment of every day, would we have fear? Would we fear how others perceive us? Would we worry about having enough material goods or not achieving worldly success? If we truly believed that God is in control and Heaven is our eternal destiny, would we still fear losing a family member or becoming ill? Would we fear loneliness or worry about how our bodies look? Would we even fear physical death?

The solution to living a life where "there is a God and I am not Him" is to become a child in that relationship. As we recall, Christ notes in the New Testament (Mt 18:3): "You must become like a child in order to enter the Kingdom of Heaven." A child has no control. A child looks fully and completely to his or her parents for everything throughout his young life. A child is completely and utterly dependent. That childlike innocence and trust allows that child to be free from worry and fear. No longer is there anxiety about tomorrow. No longer is there an unquenchable drive for wealth and power. A child simply exists… wanting to know, love and be with his parents. There is a deep peace and joy in that state of mind. A child truly lives life following the motto "There is a God and I am not Him!"

SIN

For THE PAST SEVERAL chapters we have been addressing the basic principles of the topic most people would rather avoid: sin. Sin is officially defined as "missing the mark." What does that mean? If the meaning of life is to choose God, then sin is the alternative choice. Sin is missing the mark regarding the purpose of our life. Sin is all acts, thoughts, or omissions that lead us away from our eternal destination of Heaven.

The root of all sin is pride. It is because of pride that I try to be God unto myself. It is because of pride that I often forget that "there is a God and I am not Him." It is through pride that I want control. Pride always comes before our fall from grace.

To reiterate, if God gave us our lives and our free will to choose whether or not we want to be with Him forever, then there has to be a place we could alternatively choose that would be absent of God. That alternative place is called Hell. Imagine a place where there is no Truth, no Standard, no Good, no Beauty, no Order, no Hope, no Charity, no Love, no Mercy, no Justice, and no Light. Imagine every person within this place thinking *they* were God, and, through pride, living the "religion of individualism" to its fullest. Imagine the utter loneliness in a place absent of all community. Imagine the hopelessness in a place you know will never improve for all eternity.

Many ask: If we have such a loving God, how could He ever "send" anyone to Hell? I believe that He doesn't. It is actually through His *love* for us that He has given us a free-will, to choose whether or not we want to be in His presence forever. It is because He loves us that He does not force us to be with Him. If we don't want to be with Him, we therefore choose for ourselves to be our own god and thus we choose Hell; we choose separation from Him. Remember Genesis Chapter 3 – The moment you eat of it your eyes will be open and YOU WILL BE LIKE GODS WHO KNOW WHAT IS GOOD AND WHAT IS BAD. **Remember, all who want to be God get their own kingdom absent of the true God. We call that Hell.**

My father taught me a lot about the Truth. One analogy he used made a lot of sense to me. Have you ever seen a light bulb on without a shade over it? It is really bright, even hard to look at. It also gives off heat. Imagine God is like that light bulb, always on, giving light and warmth to the world. Imagine sin is like a shade. Every time we sin we choose to place a shade on that light bulb. The light is still on but it is not quite as bright nor is it quite as warm. Then we sin again and choose to place another shade on that light. Pretty soon our spiritual relationship with the Lord becomes darker and colder. It seems to become easier for us to sin and it seems easier to place more shades on that light. Slowly but surely, we soon forget that God, The Light, is on. After putting so many shades on Him, we have now chosen a dark, cold, place for ourselves. We become accustomed to the darkness to the point where, if God is shining through another person, that light hurts our spiritual eyes and we flee from that light. That dark place is Hell.

I have met many people in my life who are already experiencing Hell, this separation from God right here on Earth. They are so enslaved by their sin that they have made a personal Hell for themselves. They become accustomed to the dark. To further understand being trapped in Hell on Earth, talk to any alcoholic or drug abuser. Talk to any person who gave up family and community for wealth and power. What you will find are individuals who are in the darkness, starving for the next fix of their addiction, feeling enslaved, alone, and utterly empty.

The good news about this life is that the light of God is still on. As long as we still have breath, there is always hope for returning to a relationship with God. It reminds me of one of Jesus' most well known parables.

"A man had two sons, and the younger son said to his father, 'Father, give me the share of your estate that should come to me.' So the father divided the property between them. After a few days, the younger son collected all his belongings and set off to a distant country where he squandered his inheritance on a life of dissipation. When he had freely spent everything, a severe famine struck that country, and he found himself in dire need. So he hired himself out to one of the local citizens who sent him to his farm to tend the swine. He longed to eat his fill of the pods on which the swine fed, but nobody gave him any. Coming to his senses he thought, 'How many of my father's hired workers have more than enough food to eat, but here am I, dying from hunger. I shall get up and go to my father and I shall say to him, "Father, I have sinned against heaven and against you. I no longer deserve to be called your son; treat me as you would treat one of your hired workers."' So he got up and went back to his father. While he was still a long way off, his father caught sight of him, and was filled with compassion. He ran to his son, embraced him and kissed him. His son said to him "Father, I have sinned against heaven and against you; I no longer deserve to be called your son." But his father ordered his servants, "Quickly bring the finest robe and put it on him; put a ring on his finger and sandals on his feet. Take the fatted calf and slaughter it. Then let us celebrate with a feast, because this son of mine was dead, and has come to life again; he was lost, and has been found." Luke 15:11

I see myself in the beginning of this parable living the "religion of individualism." This spiritual "teenager" chooses to leave his home. He decides to leave the authority of his household, to be a god unto himself. He leaves his family community and the relationship he had with his father, essentially saying he wished his father was dead so he could take his stuff.

This teenager then "set off to a distant country," leaving his land and local community. He then "squandered his inheritance on a life of dissipation" essentially choosing to end his relationship with God and leaves his religious community. He wanted control. He wanted to be God to himself. He did not want to answer to anything or anybody.

Once famine struck, he was forced to work at a pig farm in order to survive. This is ironic because, as a kosher Jew, there would be no lower place on earth than working with swine. He was not only working with the pigs, "he longed to eat his fill of the pods on which the swine fed." Symbolically, he was becoming like a pig itself, the most detestable of all mankind at that time.

It is at this moment in the story when the teenager experiences humility for the first time. Again, pride is the root of all sin. Humility is the opposite of pride. The moment this youth became more humble through self evaluation and admission of his error, he began having clarity of thought. His journey of life was instantly turned around and restarted in a positive direction. This turn-around is called *repentance*.

This teenager had the courage to act on this newfound humility and went back home. His father had never given up on him. THE LIGHT WAS STILL ON. Once the son left, the father waited, looking into the distance, hoping for his son to CHOOSE to return home. His father saw his son in the distance and ran to him and embraced him, even in his son's 'pigness.' His father was overjoyed at the return of his son and his household (Heaven) was open to him.

God is waiting for you right now. He is ready and eager to embrace each of us in our 'pigness' and welcome us into the kingdom of heaven. All that is needed is humility and the desire to 'return home.' We must become like children, innocent and trusting and longing for home.

One night my Confirmation class was giving me a really hard time. These teenagers were disrespectful, rude, and out of control. After class was over and I reflected on the evening, I seriously questioned whether or not I should continue to volunteer my time for the well-being of these kids. Nothing seemed to sink in anyway. In my exacerbation, I asked the Lord why He even bothered making teenagers. If the meaning of life is to choose God, He could have made us all in our mid-twenties and we could have gone from there. His answer back was humorous and true. He replied, "**Most people in the world are teenagers.**" In thinking of this, I realized that regardless of age, most adults have this rebellious attitude toward authority and God and are thus spiritual teenagers. To "return home," we must all become the Prodigal Son. We must perform regular self evaluation and repentance. Responding to our humility, the Lord will then give us the strength to battle our tendency to sin.

There are many different levels of sin. Some lamp shades are thicker than others. Small sins are called venial sins. This would include a white lie, not spending enough time with others, missing moments in our day when we could have helped others, swearing, and so forth. Big sins are called mortal sins. These are sins whereby the lamp shade is so thick that there is no longer any light of God in that person's life. Mortal sins are only mortal if three aspects of the action are present. First: the sin must be grave matter. This would include murder, adultery, sacrilege, and so forth. Second: the person committing the sin must know of its serious nature. Third: the individual must freely choose to do the act. One example would be a young lady forced to have an abortion. Although abortion would be grave matter, and although the young lady might know its evil, if her parents forced her to have one, she is likely not committing a mortal sin.

I am not writing this chapter because I have somehow mastered the secret of avoiding a sinful life. In reality I am one sinful guy. I am usually the guy who gets to talk to my RCIA class about sin because I am the "expert" on the subject through much experience. To let you see a bit into my twisted mind, let me tell you a story. When I was in college, I was in the confessional with a super holy priest named Fr. David Testa. He stepped foot onto my college at the Franciscan University of Steubenville as the vocational director and, as a result of his impact, that same year over 50 young men strongly considered the priesthood. He was the kind of guy that when he entered the room, you would feel the hair on your arm rising. As for me, at one point I was in the confessional with him bargaining about my sins. I wanted to know if certain sins of mine were classified as venial sins or as mortal sins. As I continued to bargain with him, he finally sat back, smiled, and stated, "**Ryan, for those who LOVE the Lord, there is no difference between venial and mortal sins, because in both cases, you are hurting your relationship with the Lord.**"

That was a profound, life-changing statement for me. Why was I always trying to do the minimum? Why did I aspire to be the guy who just sneaks into Heaven at the last minute? Had I not learned that the sin I was still hoping to pursue without significant guilt was hurting my relationship with God? As I noted before, some sins made me momentarily "happy" but would then leave a spiritual hang-over and would certainly never provide lasting joy. I was literally fighting to be able to continue having spiritual cancer in my life. What foolish justifications I have used throughout my life to continue being spiritually ill. It is like a smoker saying he is 'trying' to quit and still carries a pack of cigarettes in his pocket.

I have learned that prayer and grace from the sacraments, especially the Eucharist, are the best medicine. As a spiritual cancer patient, I look forward to the day where I can be free from this disease. In Christ I feel myself getting stronger. In my journey with Jesus, I am feeling healthier all of the time. Through Him, I will survive this spiritual disease and will have life.

GOD WILL TAKE YOU
AS YOU ARE

I AM ONE OF NINE children. One of my six sisters grew up being an all-star. She was good at everything. She got straight A's in school. She excelled socially, athletically, musically, and even spiritually. One day she tinkered with bulimia. This rapidly became a severe addiction. It put severe strains on my family financially, mentally, but especially emotionally. Everybody wanted to help her but we just couldn't find a solution. It was like witnessing a member of your family who you fiercely love drowning in your sight, not reaching up to allow you to pull her out. She was in and out of hospitals without success. She experienced guilt and started hurting herself and began to smoke as well. She began to drink alcohol daily to forget her pain. Ultimately, she entered that dark, lonely, empty place I spoke of earlier: a type of Hell. She would flee from and lash out against those with the light as the light would be blinding in her darkness. She continued on this self destructive, suicidal-like path for nearly a decade until every moment of her day was consumed by binging, purging, drinking, and smoking. She was at her absolute lowest point. She was in the state of despair. She bought into the lie of *Satan's view of her identity*: a lowly, sinful creature not worthy of God's love.

At her lowest moment I sat down to talk with her and she was finally desperate enough to listen. She told me that she believed her sins were so awful that she was convinced she was destined for Hell. I responded that the only person who was keeping her from returning to the house of the Lord was herself. What an arrogant thought to believe that the God of the universe, the God of all creation, the God of life and love wouldn't have the capacity to forgive her sins. I told her to stop fixating on her weakness and her faults and start focusing on the solution which is a relationship with the Lord. **God will take you as you are.** I told her to work on that relationship and put no priority above that. She might still be a bulimic, smoking alcoholic throughout the rest of her life until she dies but God still loves her and wants to be with her above all things. He certainly is not the one that would ever fixate on her faults. She then focused all of her energy on her relationship with Him and spent over a month in upstate New York in a Franciscan hermitage. This gave her the opportunity to be free from her physical addictions while redeveloping a relationship with God. She went through a "spiritual boot camp" there and for the first time in ten years experienced hope and the love of God. She was once again able to dive into His light and stay there. Through constant prayer and time spent in front of Jesus in Eucharistic Adoration, her demons of bulimia, smoking, and alcoholism have been controlled for many years.

I have also learned lessons of this nature at home. I have five children so far: Christopher, Trinity, Grace, Mary, and Justice. I found in raising my children that most children under age 5 want their mother, children over age 5 want their father, and children over age 12 do not want either mother or father. I formerly worked a ton of hours and would come home relatively late every evening. I found that my time was totally dominated by Christopher and Trinity, my two oldest: Dad, let me show you this; Dad, we want to play that; Dad, Dad, Dad…. I found I hardly knew my two youngest daughters or my son. The only solution I had to this was to take a weekday off work while the older children are in school and work Saturdays instead.

That has thus far been one of the most rewarding decisions I have ever made. One day I was eating my breakfast as I always do, sharing it bite for bite with my daughter Grace on my knee. I just sat there watching her eat. She was so utterly content. She had complete trust in me. She did not have a care in the entire world. She just wanted to know me, love me, and be with me like that forever. It was so simple.

At that moment I felt like how God must feel toward us. I felt totally at peace and, again, experienced true joy.

It dawned on me then why God allowed us to have children. If the meaning of life is to choose God, He could have just made us in our twenties and we could have made the "choice" for eternity and have been finished. Instead, as stated in Genesis: He made us "in His image." He allows us to co-create with Him and allows us to participate in bringing life into this world. I used to frequently ask "what does God want from me?" I think in allowing us to have a family, He has given us a pretty good clue.

God has allowed us to have children so we could have an idea about how He feels about us. Although our relationship with our children is imperfect, as our relationship with our own earthly parents was imperfect, our relationship to God is still very similar.

I want my children to be good. I want my children to be upright in character and honor. I want them to be honest, compassionate, caring, helpful, respectful, appreciative, and I want them to always try their best. I want them to live to their potential and to find lasting joy. I want them to uplift everyone around them. I want to be proud of them. I try to focus on their strengths and, if contrite, I really don't remember their weaknesses. I love them deeply. I believe I would die for them. All I really ever want from them as their father is for them to get to Heaven and *to know me, love me, and freely choose to be with me forever.* Is our Father in Heaven so different?

When my son does something at home that I am not thrilled about, I feel sad. The good news is that as long as he is at home, we can work through anything. We have a relationship where I believe he knows I would always forgive him, no matter what. There is no sin he can commit in my household that would cause me to banish him. The greatest tragedy would be if he were to ever *doubt my love* for him and choose to no longer be in my home. As welcome as he would be, he could choose to no longer continue our relationship. I couldn't force him to know me, love me, or want to be with me for eternity. I would still love him. I would long for his return.

Are you home with the Lord? Do you long to know Him, love Him, and be with Him for eternity? You still draw breath. There is still time. God will take you as you are.

THE CHURCH

AUTHORITY. IN THE REALM of religion, authority is everything. Every person and every religious institution has an opinion about Truth; the major differentiating factor between them all is authority. If we can retrace our steps a bit and recall how we arrived at this point, it would be helpful. Again, we have logically established that God exists. If He exists, there is obviously reason behind creation. He has given us clues to this reason: like the capacity to have children so we can understand His motives better. He gave us one thing to call our own—a free will—to choose where we go for eternity. He Himself came to earth as Jesus Christ to reveal to us, through example, the way to make the "perfect" choice. If you have followed this journey of logic, and accept it, then welcome to Christianity!

In this day and age, "being a Christian" is a very broad statement. This generally means that either you belong to the Catholic Church, one of 20,000 Protestant churches, or you might possibly belong to the "Church of Latter-day Saints" (Mormon faith). In my walk with the Lord, I had to carefully consider which of these paths is most consistent with the Truth espoused by Christ.

I decided that to belong to one of these churches, I needed to have faith in the authority of that church to teach the Truth. I asked myself, "If Christ is the Son of God, the Messiah, God Himself, would He have become man, revealed to us the perfect example of Truth, died on a cross, only to ascend to Heaven without leaving any authority behind to safeguard that perfect standard of Truth throughout time?"

What would have been the point of Christ if, after His ascension into Heaven, that perfect standard of Truth just left the Earth? If Christ did not leave any authority, we can imagine that much of His mission would have been in vain.

It would be like owning a family ice cream shop and making perfect ice cream. The owner of the store knows that one day he will die. Would it not be logical for the owner of the shop to find someone to replace him and pass down the recipe for making perfect ice cream? Would he not want the perfect recipe of ice cream to be passed down through ages to come? Would he allow that recipe to die with him, or would he leave *an authority* behind to ensure that the quality of his ice cream would not be diluted over time? The reality is that Jesus did leave an authority. In Mathew 16:15, Christ established the first pope.

> "He (Jesus) said to them, "But who do you say that I am?" Simon Peter said in reply, "You are the Messiah, the Son of the living God." Jesus said to him in reply, "Blessed are you, Simon son of Jonah. For flesh and blood has not revealed this to you, but my heavenly Father. And so I say to you, you are Peter, and upon this rock I will build my church, and the gates of the netherworld shall not prevail against it. I will give you the keys to the Kingdom of Heaven. Whatever you bind on earth shall be bound in heaven; and whatever you loose on earth shall be loosed in heaven."

It was Peter, filled with the Holy Spirit after Pentecost, who delivered a lengthy speech to the gathered crowd, spreading the Truth of Christ throughout the world. The entire early church, including St. Paul and all the Apostles, repeatedly deferred to the authority of Peter. One example of this was at the first council of the church, the Council of Jerusalem:

> But some from the party of the Pharisees who had become believers stood up and said, "It is necessary to circumcise them (the Gentiles) and direct them to observe the Mosaic Law." The apostles and the presbyters met

together to see about this matter. After much debate had taken place, *Peter got up and said to them*, "My brothers, you are well aware that from early days God made his choice among you that through my mouth the Gentiles would hear the word of the gospel and believe. And God, who knows the heart bore witness by granting them the Holy Spirit just as he did us. He made no distinction between us and them, for by faith he purified their hearts. Why, then, are you now putting God to the test by placing on the shoulders of the disciples a yoke that neither our ancestors nor we have been able to bear? On the contrary, we believe that we are saved through the grace of the Lord Jesus, in the same way as they. The whole assembly fell silent, and they listened while Paul and Barnabas described the signs and wonders God had worked among the Gentiles through them." Acts 15: 5-12.

As this passage from the Acts of the Apostles demonstrates, there was much debate, but then *Peter spoke* and the debate was immediately settled. Within the Catholic Church, since Jesus himself gave Peter the "keys to Heaven and Earth," there has been an authority that has remained throughout history; we call that authority "the pope." The person who presently "sits in Peter's chair" for the church is Pope Benedict XVI. The Catholic bishops are the present day apostles. These bishops have an apostolic lineage of authority that has been passed down through the generations from Peter and the first apostles till now.

There have been several councils of the Church over the past 2000 years. All these councils have been similar to that first Council of Jerusalem. There is normally a topic of faith which requires debate and clarification but, in the end, when statements are made by the bishops in union with the pope, a Catholic can have faith in the Truth set forth by these councils. In the teaching of faith and morals, there are always consistent teachings. We can have faith in the Church because of the Church's authority. Without authority, there is only opinion.

The Catholic Church has three "pillars of faith." A pillar of faith is used to reveal the fullness of the Truth on Earth. All three pillars of faith work in unison and are never contradictory. The first pillar of faith is the Magesterium of the Church. This is the teaching authority discussed above which includes the bishops in union with the pope. The members of this group are the shepherds Christ put in charge to guide His Church until His Second Coming.

The second pillar of faith is the Tradition of the Church. This Tradition is the collection of teachings and customs passed from generation to generation to maintain the words and actions of Jesus—to maintain that "perfect ice cream recipe." This Tradition was maintained through oral history for years and existed before the gospels were written and the Bible and New Testament were constructed. This Tradition includes all the divine revelation captured and collected so that every generation of Catholics doesn't have to "reinvent the wheel." There is a significant advantage to having the ability to theologically stand on the shoulders of giants.

Finally, the third pillar of faith is Scripture itself. The Catholic Church believes the Bible is divinely inspired. As Christ recognized the authority of Scripture, so do Catholics.

It is through the combination and union of these "pillars of faith" that the Catholic Church boldly claims to have the "fullness of the Truth." This is not to say that other religions do not contain some Truth. However, some of these religions contain more Truth than others. But the Truth found in these faiths is ultimately the Truth already recognized by the Catholic Church.

Our Protestant brothers and sisters also have a significant amount of Truth in their faith. Many of my closest friends and relatives come from a Protestant background. (Note that I use the word "Protestant" to refer to all non-Catholic Christians.) I have truly learned a lot from these brothers and sisters in Christ. I do not doubt their faith or relationship with the Lord. Too often I am a coward. For the sake of comfort, I miss the opportunity to question my friends on what they actually believe and why. What is funny is that most of these non-Catholic Christians don't really know what our differences are. Too many times I have missed an opportunity to truly question why we Christians are still divided. Do we not all believe in a Lord of unity? Do we not believe that God desires a unified "Body of Christ?"

At times there are Catholics who attend a local Protestant church service and are impressed with the warm and inviting community atmosphere. There is significant love for Christ in these churches and a significant love for one another. It is this feeling of warmth, coupled with the lack of understanding of their own faith, that cause some Catholics to leave their Catholic Faith for another Christian church. There were times in my walk with the Lord that I thought about converting to a church that was more "active" than my own, or where I liked the music or the preaching better. I would then search for the authority of that church and would discover a great, beautiful, entertaining church built on a foundation of sand. I would then inevitably turn my gaze back to Peter "the Rock" and know that I was home.

The word Protestant is actually rooted in the word "protest." The Protestants are in "protest" of the Catholic Church. This protest started in the middle ages when a Catholic priest, Martin Luther, left the church because he was "protesting" the actions of his regional bishop at the time. His concerns with the abuse of power of his bishop were well founded. Although the Magesterium has the authority of Christ, that certainly doesn't mean that Christ's shepherds are perfect disciples. I often must remind myself that priests and bishops are still human and thus still sinners.

I then remind myself of who Christ picked to be his first Apostles. He picked a bunch of misfits. When you think about it, the first pope of the Church ate and drank with Christ regularly for years. He witnessed first-hand the miracles of the Savior. He boldly allowed himself to be led by the Holy Spirit on numerous occasions. Ultimately, when the moment of truth arrived, Peter denied Christ three times. This betrayal was similar to the betrayal of Judas. The only difference between these two betrayers of Jesus is that Judas believed his sin was "too big for God" and fell into despair. Judas forgot who should be in control; he forgot who was God. In his dark and cold world, where he, Judas, was god, there was no humility, no forgiveness. He felt he had only one way out—he hung himself.

Peter took the opposite approach. After betraying Christ, he recognized his weakness in humility and repented to God. His soul was saved. It is through weak and humble men like Peter that Christ chose to entrust the survival of His legacy: His Church.

Dr. Scott Hahn often makes a good point: if one has a medical physician that smokes and weighs 350 pounds, doesn't the medicine that the Doctor prescribes still work to heal physical disease? This concept applies to spiritual health as well. Although our Catholic priests are not always perfect, would it not make sense that the spiritual medicine they provide us through the Sacraments still works to heal our spiritual disease?

Although many of our priests are weak men, a vast majority have a singular purpose to their life. That purpose is to bring me and you and everyone they encounter to Heaven by teaching us about Christ and giving us "manna for the journey" through the sacraments. These educated men have sacrificed everything for us. They have given up control of their destiny to their superiors. They have given up a worldly family so they could offer us, the sheep, more of their attention. They have died unto themselves for you and me. How often I take for granted their presence in my life. How often I have missed the opportunity to thank them for their sacrifice.

The fundamental problem with Martin Luther rejecting the Church was that, instead of focusing specifically on the abuses he saw with the practical management of the Church, he started to change his core beliefs in the realm of faith and morals to his own liking. His new religion was so uniquely his own, it ultimately came to be called the Luther-an church. He eliminated the first two "pillars of faith" all together and he, like the 20,000 other protestant denominations, believe in only one pillar of faith: that of Scripture alone.

What Luther failed to recognize is that oral Tradition came before Scripture. It was only after the Apostles recognized that the Second Coming of Christ was not likely to occur in their lifetime that the gospels were finally written down. It was the Catholic Church that decided during the Council of Trent which books of the Bible were "divinely inspired" and therefore included.

By eliminating the belief in any authority and using Scripture alone, Martin Luther set up a system inclined to perpetuate continuous division because people interpret Scripture differently. Without a Magesterium to provide an interpretation of Scripture consistent with Tradition, a Protestant church may thrive only as long as its pastor is present. The moment that pastor leaves, or there is a disagreement or debate about the interpretation of Scripture within that church because there is no authority or tradition, there is a risk that the church will break down into more protestant sects. That is why there are currently over 20,000 different Protestant churches in the United States. Even within the Lutheran faith, one Lutheran service may be different from another Lutheran service that takes place down the street because again, the entire Protestant faith is based primarily upon the interpretation of Scripture by the individual pastor. The Bible was and is a source of Truth. However, without the context of tradition since the time of Christ, and without the shepherds in the Magesterium to guide the flock, the sheep will interpret Scripture as they see fit. The Truth is then dependent upon the views of the individual pastor or some kind of democratic process with a group of "elders."

The reason why many Protestant churches seem to be "on fire with the Spirit" is because most of these churches are first or second generation churches. Most of the people in the church have freely chosen to be there for a reason. The question about the teaching message given in a church—beyond all the bells and whistles—is what the church looks like after four or five generations when the members have not freely chosen to join the church on their own accord but were born into the faith. A church without a strong consistent message based in Truth cannot stand the test of time when the initial zeal has died along with its original members.

Do you really think that the Truth of the universe is based on a democratic process? Would Christ have intended on leaving a church with these continuous divisions? Would Christ have left us without a Shepherd? Would He have expected us to individually come to the Truth ourselves without taking into consideration the Truths found by our forefathers? Do we believe we are really the first ones to come up with questions about our faith? Do we believe that no one else throughout Christian history has come up with any answers? Was Jesus wrong when He stated that "the netherworld will not prevail against it (the Church)?"

At the end of the day, I believe a lot of protestant Christians frequently *act* upon the "Truths" established by the Catholic Church better than some Catholics, whether the Protestant recognizes this reality or not. We are all truly brothers and sisters in Christ. If you are a non-Catholic Christian, I implore you to discover the origins of your protestant sect. I ask that you look for the authority of your faith. When you find that it does not originate historically with Christ Himself, I implore you to consider returning home to the Catholic family. There are so many people that look at us (Christians) as the enemy. Now, more than ever before, we need to stand as one. I look forward to the day when all Christians are once again unified in the "Fullness of the Truth."

THE CROSS

WHILE RAISING MY CHILDREN, I have found that one of the most important roles I play in their life is to help guide them into making healthy spiritual decisions. Part of that guidance is through discipline. If they harm their siblings physically, emotionally, or mentally, they are given consequences. These consequences range from a verbal check, to 'time out,' to grounding, and yes, rarely even a spanking. I never *want* to punish my children. Frankly, punishing my children is my least favorite thing to do in the whole world. I use discipline to guide them because I love them. I want them to be aware of how their decisions affect others and the community as a whole. I want them to realize that there are consequences to most decisions they will make day to day. I want them to grow up with a sense of justice. In the end, my children fear (respect) me as their father, and they are also aware of my fierce love of them. They know I would give my entire being to help guide them to eternity with God. They know I would die for them. In this, the love that is returned to me is deep and lasting. Do you believe our Father in Heaven is so different?

Why was atonement for our sins necessary? It is because we have a God who is just. Our sin committed has eternally challenged infinite justice. With our first sin, there was injury to an eternal, infinite relationship between man and God. There must be a consequence to our action, not because of what Adam and Eve did in sin, but because of Whom it is they offended by that sin. Their sin created an eternal chasm in the relationship between man and God because God is infinite.

Do you believe God is infinite? Do you believe God is just? Do you believe in God's mercy? Our forefathers believed in these attributes of God. In the Old Testament, after the fall of man through the first sin of Adam and Eve, man routinely offered sacrifice to God. This was true with Abel, Abraham, and Moses. Why did man sacrifice? It is through the blood of the sacrifice that man would receive finite (temporary) atonement for their sin. The reason the sacrifice was temporal was that we were sacrificing finite animals to atone for *in*finite Justice. The only sacrifice that can truly satisfy infinite or divine justice would be if our atonement was made through divine sacrifice. That divine sacrifice could only be given by God alone. According to Dr. Scott Hahn, "God would have to pay a debt He did not owe because man owed a debt he could not pay."

Jesus Christ had a two-fold mission on this planet. As we have discussed, He came down from Heaven to show us the "perfect choice." As the Way, the Truth, and the Life, Christ provided a roadmap of healthy behavior in order for us to foster a relationship with God the Father and hopefully join Him throughout eternity.

The second and equally important mission of Christ was to be the Divine Sacrifice. In the person of Jesus Christ, and through his crucifixion and resurrection, God has once again revealed His justice, mercy, and love.

The other day I was watching a television program on National Geographic about the universe. The program first noted that satellites we deployed over twenty years ago are just now reaching the fringes of our solar system. To put the size of our solar system to scale, it was noted that if our solar system was the size of an average DVD, then the size of the diameter of the planet Earth relative to the size of the DVD would be proportionate to the size of our galaxy to our solar system. Even more amazing is that the universe has billions of known galaxies. There is thought to be more stars in the universe than grains of sand on the entire Earth. The magnitude of the universe is incomprehensible to our human brain.

Thinking about these facts reminds me about how small I am. I am like an ant—no, even less. I am like the smallest particle of dust.

I spent this past Christmas meditating on the reality that the God of this universe, the God of these billions of galaxies and trillions of stars, loved me so much that He became man: God became dust. Not only did the God of the universe become dust, He allowed Himself to be born in a stable: He allowed Himself to be the lowest form of dust. I, like the myriads of angels, shepherds, wise men, Joseph and Mary, can only stand in wonderment at the humility of this God.

Not only did God become dust, but He allowed this dust to torture Him, and ultimately to hang Him on a cross. I simply cannot conceive of the degree of love God has for me. This whole story seems really insane. It goes well beyond my reasoning capacity to try and remotely grasp the insane love that God has for me. I sit and stare at the cross and, in the end, I can only praise Him.

What is even more insane is that this God of the universe would have completed this mission if it were to only save *me*. Christ frequently talks about a shepherd dropping everything to search for one lost sheep. It is much like the God of the universe dropping everything to make sure He found *me* and brought *me* home.

I imagine Satan tormenting in Jesus the Garden of Gethsemane on the eve before His death, whispering in his ear, "Are you sure you want to go through with this? Think of how many people will not accept the grace of your divinely shed blood as a result of their pride and self conceit. You will be tortured and crucified in vain. The souls of these 'children of God' are mine."

I imagine Christ at that moment, defiantly resisting temptation as He thought of you and me, hoping in our choice for salvation. It is thoughts like this that cause me to find myself madly in love with Jesus Christ, *my* Savior.

Christ did not die to fulfill some abstract distant idea. He died for *ME*! In *my* sin He allowed *me* to beat Him. He stood still as I scourged the flesh from His body. He didn't fight back when I slapped Him. He stood with utter dignity as I spit in His face. He didn't cry out as I pressed a crown of thorns into His scalp. He simply closed His eyes when I drove nails through His hands and feet. He looked into my eyes as I raised Him up to suffocate on that cross.

It is through this same cross that He wipes away the tears from my soul. It is through His shed blood that He forgives me, embraces me, kisses me, and welcomes me home to the eternal feast. I love Him, I love Him, I love Him.

HOLY COMMUNION

I HAVE LEARNED THAT GOD has given us a time machine that brings us back in time to witness first-hand the Last Supper of Jesus Christ and His crucifixion. We can literally eat and drink with Christ and physically stand at the foot of the cross, gazing upon the Savior who is dying for our sins. We can then come into union with Him, becoming *one* with His resurrected body, blood, soul, and divinity. We can also become *one* with the Church family through the same Communion. We can do this today, right now, at any Mass held throughout the world.

When I was growing up, I always looked at the Mass as a *meal* in which the "Body of Christ," the Church, gathers to build community. I believed that the meal shared at church with the 'Church family' was similar to the meal I shared at home with my family. This is, in fact, true. Mealtime is a critically important opportunity to share with one another, to learn about one another, to encourage each other, to learn about our Faith, to strengthen relationships, and to grow more unified as a family. I can tell you that there is no time more precious at home than the meal time I spend with my family. However, what I discovered in college is that, while this type of community building occurs at each Mass, the essence of Mass is much, much deeper and incredibly profound. I had not yet remotely grasped the magnitude of what actually occurs in this Sacrament of Holy Communion.

The Mass has its roots all the way back to the book of Genesis with Abraham. In short, Abraham desperately wanted a son. He was obedient to God and God established a covenant (a contract) with Abraham. As a result of Abraham's obedience, God promised Abraham "descendants as numerous as the stars."(Gen15:5) Ultimately, Isaac was born. Abraham loved "his only beloved son."

As the story continued, Abraham's faith and obedience was put to the test. The Lord asked Abraham to sacrifice "his only beloved son."

Genesis 22:1-13

Sometime after these events, God put Abraham to the test. He called to him, "Abraham!" "Ready!" he replied. Then God said: "Take your son Isaac, your only one, whom you love, and go to the land of Moriah. There you shall offer him up as a holocaust on a height that I will point out to you…Thereupon Abraham *took the wood for the holocaust and laid it on his son Isaac's shoulders,* while he himself carried the fire and the knife. As the two walked on together, Isaac spoke to his father Abraham: "Father!" he said. "Yes, son," he replied. Isaac continued, "Here are the fire and the wood, but where is the lamb for the holocaust?" "Son," Abraham answered, *"God himself will provide the lamb for the holocaust."* Then the two continued forward. When they came to the place of which God told him, Abraham built an altar there and arranged the wood on it. Next he tied up his son Isaac, and put him on top of the wood on the altar. Then he reached out and took the knife to slaughter his son. But the Lord's messenger called to him from heaven, "Abraham, Abraham!" "Yes Lord," he answered. "Do not lay your hand on the boy," said the messenger. "Do not do the least thing to him. I know now how devoted you are to God, since you did not withhold from me your own beloved son." As Abraham looked about, he spied a ram caught by its horns in the thicket. So he went and took the ram and offered it up as a holocaust in place of his son.

This concept of a beloved son carrying wood on his shoulders and being sacrificed sounds a lot like the crucifixion of Jesus Christ. Considering the reality that Isaac was large enough to carry the wood of the sacrifice on his shoulders and that his father, Abraham, was an old man, Isaac likely offered himself to be bound prior to the sacrifice. The Jews built Solomon's temple on the traditional site of where that event occurred. When the Jews sacrificed the unblemished lambs in the temple, a ram's horn was blown to remind God that "He will provide the lamb (Jesus Christ)." When John the Baptist first saw Jesus, he boldly proclaimed "Behold the Lamb of God that takes away the sins of the world."(Jn1:29)

The Jewish Passover is another example of the tradition of the "sacrifice of the lamb." In Exodus 12:3-8 we find the verse:

"Tell the whole community of Israel: On the tenth of this month every one of your families must procure a lamb...The lamb must be a year old and without blemish. You may take it from either the sheep or the goats. You shall keep it until the fourteenth day of this month, and then, with the whole assembly of Israel present, it shall be slaughtered during the evening twilight. They shall take some of its blood and apply it to the two doorposts and the lintel of every house in which they partake of the lamb. That same night *they shall eat its roasted flesh with unleavened bread* and bitter herbs."

On Palm Sunday, Christians celebrate Jesus entering Jerusalem. Historically it happened to be the same day that the "unblemished" lambs were likewise being ushered to the temple. At the Passover meal itself the following Thursday evening, Jesus took the unleavened bread "said the blessing, broke it, and giving it to his disciples said, "Take and eat; this is my body." Then he took a cup, gave thanks, and gave it to them, saying, "Drink from it, all of you, for this is my blood of the covenant, which will be shed on behalf of many for the forgiveness of sins." (Mt 26:26-28)

It was at the Passover meal that Christ gave Himself to be consumed: body, blood, soul, and divinity just as the Jews would normally consume the slaughtered, unblemished lamb, not only for Passover but also to seal a new covenant.

It was immediately after this Passover meal (the Last Supper) that Christ was taken into custody and condemned. The next day, he was hanging on the cross at the same time that the unblemished lambs of Passover were being slaughtered in the temple. It is believed that Christ died at 3:00 PM.

While I was growing up, I somehow separated in my head the Last Supper event from the Passion: that is, the suffering and death of Christ. In Truth, **the Last Supper is the Passion!** Christ truly is "the Lamb of God." The major difference is that, because Christ is divine, His sacrifice pays the price for our sin and satisfies divine justice.

At every "sacrifice of the Mass," we follow what Christ commanded for us. He stated after the consecration in Luke 22:19, "Do this in memory of me." At Mass we re-present the sacrifice of the divine Son to His Father in Heaven. Think about it. We enter church and we purify ourselves by repenting of our sins. We say a prayer of contrition called the Confiteor:

> I confess to almighty God, and to you, my brothers and sisters, that I have sinned through my own fault, in my thoughts and in my words, in what I have done, and what I have failed to do; and I ask Blessed Mary, ever virgin, all of the Angels and Saints, and you, my brothers and sisters, to pray for me to the Lord our God.

Then, as the Jews did formerly, we bring our monetary gifts to the altar. As one "Body of Christ," we offer the only thing that we have that is our own: we offer to God *our will.* We sacrifice our control. We offer up our daily sufferings, our crosses. We give over to God our desire for all things other than Heaven. We put these sacrifices, these gifts, on the altar along with the Son of Man with the fervent anticipation that the covenant that God the Father has with all of us is about to be renewed.

The Catholic priest washes his hands as would the Jewish priest before he slaughtered the unblemished lamb. On the altar, the priest offers the Body of Christ and the Blood of Christ *separately* to the

Father. (At the last supper Christ did not say this is my body *and* my blood.) When the blood is separated from the body, one is dead.

This moment of offering, this moment of consecration, is the moment we are mystically and physically present at the cross: the same cross as 2000 years ago; the same cross that transcends time with this sacrifice; the same cross that saved me from separation from God and allows me to be able to "come home" to the Lord when the time of my eternal choice comes to an end. It is through the reception of this "Passover" sacrifice that the blood of Christ, the Lamb of God, is wiped on the doorposts of my soul and the "Angel of Death" can no longer affect my destiny.

At Mass, we then proclaim, "Christ has died, Christ is risen, Christ will come again." At this moment, we are in the presence of the living, resurrected God in the form of this unleavened bread and wine which has been transformed into the actual Body and Blood of Christ.

We then consume Jesus and, if we are in the state of grace (without mortal sin), we become *one* with Him and *one* in communion with the community of believers; we become *one* with the "Body of Christ." I have often told our widows not to concern themselves at length with visiting their deceased spouse in the cemetery as they can still become *one* with them at Mass.

In becoming one with Christ, we are given "manna for the journey" of life. The Jews sustained themselves physically on manna (unleavened bread) in the desert. I sustain myself spiritually on manna from heaven: Jesus Christ. In receiving Him, I have the potential to receive an abundance of spiritual grace that sustains me and helps me to make choices for God. In receiving Christ, the Lord gives to me all the grace I am open to, and capable of, receiving. How can one receive grace greater than the body and blood of the Son of Man?

If you have doubt about the true and complete presence of Christ in the Eucharist, you are not alone. If you were to ever memorize a verse from Scripture, the following would be the one to remember. My Protestant friends who seem to have the entire Bible memorized chapter and verse generally leave me alone after we discuss John 6:47-69:

"Amen, Amen I say to you, whoever believes has eternal life. I am the Bread of Life. Your ancestors ate the manna in the desert and they died; this is the bread that comes down from Heaven so that one may eat it and not die. I am the Living Bread that came down from Heaven; whoever eats this bread will live forever; and the bread that I will give is my flesh for the life of the world." The Jews quarreled among themselves, saying, "How can this man give us his flesh to eat?" Jesus said to them, "Amen, Amen I say to you, unless you eat of the flesh of the Son of Man and drink his blood, you do not have life within you. Whoever eats My flesh and drinks My blood has eternal life, and I will raise him on the last day. For My flesh is true food, and My blood is true drink. Whoever eats My flesh and drinks My blood remains in Me and I in him. This is the bread that came down from Heaven. Unlike your ancestors who ate and still died, whoever eats this bread will live forever." Then many of his disciples who were listening said "This saying is hard; who can accept it?"...As a result of this, many of his disciples returned to their way of life and no longer accompanied Him. Jesus then said to the Twelve, "Do you also want to leave?" Simon Peter answered Him, "Master, to whom shall we go? You have the words of eternal life. We have come to believe and are convinced that you are the Holy One of God."

Jesus never said the Eucharist was a *symbol* of anything. He was so specific about this Truth that He was willing to allow all of His followers, including His twelve Apostles to leave Him. His closest friends, His apostles, didn't understand at the time what the Lord was talking about. Peter (as usual) states, "To whom shall we go?" They had faith without understanding.

Often I have asked myself about this Truth, that is, the true presence of God in this cup of wine or this piece of unleavened bread. In my doubt I ask myself one question, "Where else would I go?" I have accepted the fact that, in this case like many others, I do not know everything or understand everything. I am a spiritual child. I have faith that my Church, my spiritual mother, has my best interests at heart. Like a mother, to the extent I can understand, it is her goal to teach me Truth.

When my children were two years of age, I would tell them that the stove was hot. No matter how much the two year old would argue about it, or will it to be otherwise, the stove remained hot. My children didn't have to believe it, or understand it to be true, in order for the hotness of the stove to be reality. Ultimately, if they disobeyed me and touched the stove, they got burned.

My spiritual mother, the Church, is the same. Based on her knowledge of Christ and her 2000 years of collective experience, the Church has a thorough grasp of the difference between *healthy* spiritual behavior versus *unhealthy* spiritual behavior. Like my worldly mother, the Church remains with me as a support to comfort me if I touch the hot, spiritual stove and get spiritually burned.

I am not recommending that one remain ignorant about *why* the Church teaches what it does. Through asking questions, I can mature in my faith. I can learn to obey not out of fear that the stove is hot, but rather, I learn to obey because I love my mother. This is how a mature relationship with the Lord and His Church can be achieved. But in the end, I try to obey my mother first, and then later I work to understand the "why" of things when the Lord determines the appropriate time to teach me.

The other objective of my mother Church is to feed me and support me through my journey of life by providing the grace offered through the sacraments. It is through the reception of Christ in Holy Communion (the Eucharist), that I am spiritually nourished. The Church recommends that, as long as I am in a "state of grace" (that is, without mortal sin), I should be spiritually nourished at least once a week on the Sabbath (Sunday).

Upon reflection, however, if I were to eat food only once per week, my body would be sustained but it would be starving. Likewise, receiving the Eucharist once per week sustains my soul, but my soul hungers for more! Why not take the opportunity go back in time to be with my Lord at His cross and resurrection every day at daily Mass? Why not practice healthy spiritual living?

Christ is truly present at every Mass, in every country throughout the world, every day. It doesn't matter if the priest is boring, old, young, mean, fantastic, holy, crazy, or even speaks your language. Nothing else matters other than the fact that *Christ Himself* is there. The Angels of Heaven kiss the fingers of your priest as he holds in his hands the body, blood, soul, and divinity of God. These Angels do not discriminate who the priest is because Christ is present; that is all that matters. I go to Mass to receive Christ. The specific celebrant of the Mass is irrelevant to me.

The kids in my Confirmation class often comment that Mass is "boring." I would then explain that God didn't put His cross in our presence to entertain us. I don't attend Mass to be entertained. Rather, I attend Mass to be in the *presence of God* when He suffers and dies for my sins. Once the kids understand that the center of the universe, the ground zero of salvation, is based on this sacrifice of the cross present at every Mass; once they understand they are to offer themselves on that same altar; then Mass is no longer viewed as some form of entertainment, but the truest reality.

It is the grace of the cross, the grace of every Mass, which unites Heaven to Earth. As much as God is present to us all the time, by coming to us body, blood, soul, and divinity, God is uniquely present to us at Mass. Once I understood the Truth about God's real presence at Mass, my behavior changed. There is no earthly priority that can even come close to the priority of that cross. Sleep, sports, family events, shopping, work, and school—*nothing* is more important to my salvation than the reception of Christ at Mass. If what I am doing is not benefiting my journey to salvation, I am wasting my time. I am forgetting the meaning of my life.

When I go to meet God, I try to respect Who it is I am about to receive. I fast from food one hour prior to Mass. I try to arrive early and I don't rush out at the end. I genuflect (kneel) toward the tabernacle before entering the pew and when leaving the church. I dress appropriately for Mass in respect for the Lord who has invited me to His house. I try to focus on what is transpiring at Mass, especially during the consecration. In giving of myself completely in sacrifice, I offer to the Lord my voice at Mass and expect my kids, with voices good and bad, to do the same. I kneel upright throughout the consecration and bow my head respectfully at the consecration itself. I also bow just before receiving Christ in the Eucharist. Also, as I have become more mature in my faith, I now receive Jesus directly on my tongue rather touch Him with my hands. My intention in doing this is to be as respectful as possible.

I also realize that I need to be ready spiritually to receive Christ. If I have mortal sin on my soul, the act of receiving Christ prior to the repentance of that sin in the sacrament of Confession is a *sacrilege* (a serious sin caused by the irreverent act). If I am not prepared to receive Christ, I must still attend Mass to be with my church family. Again, the only person keeping me out of grace is myself. God wants me home. He even wants me home if I am covered in sin. As I mentioned before, all venial (non-serious) sin is forgiven upon the reception of the Eucharist.

The Lord loves to be present fully to His children at the Mass. One evening my youngest sister (as an adult) decided she was going to sleep late and miss Mass the following morning. I told her, "The Lord expects you to be at Mass." She laughed and said, "Prove it." I said, "God will wake you up and not allow you to fall back asleep." She is a very deep sleeper and didn't take my comment seriously. The next morning, true to my prophecy, a large fly buzzed around her room and landed repeatedly on her sleeping face. It finally bothered her enough that she got up in time for Mass and decided to attend. She later thanked me for 'kicking her in the butt' and has attended Mass at least weekly since then.

The time machine God has given to all of us is such a blessing. To be back in time with Christ at the time of his death we have the opportunity to truly know Him "through the breaking of the bread."(Lk 24:35)

PRAYER

I HAVE FOUND IN MY short life that, in every relationship, communication is paramount. This is especially true in the family. I have observed that there are countless technological tools we use which, despite their obvious value, contribute to a breakdown in real human to human communication. Like many of you, I have ready access to the media, TV, radios, computers, I-pods, Blackberrys, and so forth. These worldly gadgets really distract me from being present to my immediate environment. Just ask my wife. When I engage in a video game or TV show, for example, I find that I am not present to my wife and children. With that constant electronic buzz in my head, it is nearly impossible to hear the Lord communicating to me through my family and my environment. Fortunately, now that I'm more aware, I'm making some progress. I've gotten rid of many distractions. However, I continue to struggle with my addiction to TV.

Without communication, relationships die. Just ask any divorcee or child distant from a parent. I have found that my relationship with God is no different. Without prayer, it would be like telling the Lord, "I love you. I will give up everything for you. I just don't want to talk to you."

Prayer is simply communication with the Lord. This communication doesn't mean I always need to use words. Sometimes I just sit with my wife. We don't need to talk about anything. We just hold hands and sit together. We are *present* to one another. This communicates to her that she is important to me. This lets her know that there is nothing more important to me at that moment than her.

Similarly, I sometimes just sit with the Lord in what is called Adoration of the Eucharist. To enable Adoration, a consecrated Communion Host—that is, the body, blood, soul, and divinity of Jesus Christ—is placed by the Catholic priest in a transparent receptacle called a monstrance. The real presence of Jesus Christ is thereby visible to me. At that point, I just sit in His presence. Sometimes I talk; sometimes I listen. In all cases, being with Him in person is like getting a suntan of grace. There is something special about stopping my life for a moment to simply *be* with the Lord. Like taking a pilgrimage, God seems to appreciate the effort. He rewards my life with peace and joy, no matter how tough things of the world are. Now that doesn't mean I don't have normal anxiety about my worldly responsibilities. In prayer, God simply re-centers my priorities and gives me the grace to endure.

In many ways, my whole life is a prayer. Each morning I offer up my day to the Lord to do with me as He wills. I offer up the challenges He places before me and I ask for the wisdom to never miss an opportunity to bring others to Him. I live my life with an acute awareness that *there are no accidents*. I accept the current moment and try to learn from every situation the Lord brings me.

In my journey of life, I often reflect on my day and ask God to identify those areas in me that need the most correction and healing. I have so many weaknesses. However, with the insight God gives me, I am able to focus my prayer and ask for the grace (spiritual medicine) to address my specific spiritual illness.

Other than the Mass itself, the greatest prayer I have ever encountered is the prayer of the rosary. The rosary is organized prayer. This prayer primarily consists of repeating the "Hail Mary" and the "Our Father." The secret of the rosary is that each decade of the rosary (one Our Father and ten Hail Mary's) is associated with a specific timeframe in Christ's life. These are broken down into the Joyful Mysteries, the Luminous Mysteries, the Sorrowful Mysteries, and the Glorious Mysteries. For example, to pray the rosary of the Sorrowful Mysteries, one contemplates respectively during each decade one of the following five mysteries: the agony in the garden, the scourging at the pillar, the crowning with thorns, the carrying of the cross, and the crucifixion.

The recitation of this organized prayer, the rosary, allows my mind to meditate on the important events in the life of Jesus. Meanwhile, as I am meditating on the life of Jesus, I am also asking Mary, the mother of Jesus and my spiritual mother, to intercede for us and pray for us "now and at the hour of our death." It is important to point out that we are not praying "to" Mary, as if she is God. She was human, like you and me. However, she had and has a very unique role and responsibility. While on one hand, she is merely another member of the Mystical Body of Christ, the Church, she is on the other hand the "heart." Christ is the "head." We are the little toe. She is the conduit of life-giving divine "blood" (grace) to us.

Praying the rosary is a powerful spiritual weapon. Satan hates it. I start praying the rosary at times when I am tempted; there seems to be nothing more effective in refocusing my mind on my master and friend, Jesus Christ. It is a prayer that opens a font of grace in my life.

Let me tell you a secret. I really don't enjoy praying the rosary. It takes a lot of discipline. The rosary is a spiritual *exercise*.

I also don't like physical exercise. There is nothing I like to do less than run on a treadmill. However, I do it because it makes me physically healthy. After I work out, I feel great. I feel physically fast and alert and ready for the physical challenges of that day. If I miss my regular workout, I feel physically slow and dull and out of shape when I am physically challenged that day.

Praying the rosary is similar to that physical exercise. When I pray the rosary, I feel great. I feel spiritually fast and alert and ready for the spiritual challenges I will encounter that day. If I miss the rosary, I feel spiritually slow and dull and spiritually out of shape, not ready to face any spiritual challenges I am bound to encounter that day.

I found that I use the time in my day when I would otherwise be doing nothing else and pray the rosary then. This is most often for me while driving. That is the time when the rosary is the most palatable for me and I am able to successfully do it.

I used to be resistant to organized rote prayers, such as the "Hail Mary" and the "Our Father." I thought to myself, "if I were trying to cultivate a relationship with my wife and kids, and they started to talk to me in some type of prepared speech all of the time, my relationship probably wouldn't be strengthened much by that."

That way of thinking is somewhat valid. If my prayer life was simply a robotic routine of organized prayer alone; if I never made any personal connection to Jesus or accepted His sacrifice for me personally, then my relationship with Him wouldn't be a relationship at all. It would *only* be a religious routine. If I never talked to the Lord using normal conversation, I would have an impersonal relationship with my God.

On the other hand, when I have the discipline to set aside the time to pray with organized prayer—when I have spiritual discipline—I find that I will simply talk to the Lord more often than I might otherwise. Without that spiritual discipline, I often become spiritually apathetic. I get so caught up with the routine of life that I simply forget to talk to the Lord. There are also times when I simply don't have much to say.

These are the times that we can say the prayer Jesus Christ Himself taught us, the Our Father or ask Mary, our spiritual mother, to pray with us. These prayers are crucial for our spiritual journey and provide us grace: the spiritual nudge to make the right choices for God.

In the end, making time each day to start with the spiritual exercise of organized prayer can lead to more time when a spontaneous conversation can occur. It is like going on a date with my wife. We can talk at home anytime we want, but in the chaos of the home life, we can go days without a focused conversation. Fortunately we then have the relationship discipline to regularly stop our routine, go out on a date, and just *be with* each other. We may or may not have a productive conversation every time, but, by going on a date, we are giving ourselves a specific time when a great conversation can occur. In all cases, a date is healthy for our relationship.

A disciplined prayer life is like going on a date with the Lord. It is a time in the day that I set aside and I pray my organized prayer. Sometimes this leads to spontaneous prayer; sometimes it does not. In all cases, organized prayer is healthy for our relationship.

There is no greater place to experience the combination of both organized and spontaneous prayer than the Mass itself. At any Catholic Church I might attend throughout the world, at any given moment, the essential prayers are consistent at the Mass and the format is essentially the same everywhere. It is truly the "Mystical Body of Christ" speaking and praying in one voice to the Father, "Remember the sacrifice of your only son. Remember your covenant to us through His divine blood."

There are times during the Mass when we pray spontaneously. This is most evident around the time of receiving Jesus in the Eucharist. This is the moment of my life when I am truly closest to God and I pour my soul out to Him. Mass is the cornerstone of my prayer life. It is central to my life, the life of my family, and the life of my spiritual wellbeing. There is no prayer that is more important or that provides more grace. In Mass, my prayer transcends words and thoughts. In receiving the Eucharist (Christ's body, blood, soul, and divinity), my entire being, including my physical being, is in prayer to the Lord. He is *in* me, and I am *in* Him. It is similar to the deep communication, the deep communion, which occurs between a man and wife during the marital act. It is a complete and total giving of all aspects of self: mental, emotional, spiritual, and physical. There is no deeper communication than that.

Through prayer, the Lord has changed my life. He gives me ideas, answers questions, gives me tasks to accomplish, and reminds me of His love for me. I pray right now that the Lord remain with me during this current task. I pray that I write what He desires me to write. I ask for His blessing to rain down on all the readers of this book. I pray that we can all experience His peace and presence now and through all eternity. Amen.

MARY

I TRULY LOOK FORWARD TO teaching RCIA (the Rite of Christian Initiation of Adults) when I get to introduce the class attendees to their spiritual mother. I have the same type of excitement now when I get to introduce you to her as well. To me, it is like finding a child who lost their mother in some tragedy, and then helping to reunite them.

I was introduced to my spiritual mother in the eighth grade. At that time one of my older sisters was the family rebel. She was a typical teenager, depressed and angry at the world. Most of that anger was directed at my parents. She seemed compelled to break every rule my parents made. She was clearly searching for something, or *someone*—for what or for whom, she had only the faintest idea.

She ultimately read a book about Medjugorje, Yugoslavia, where the Blessed Mother was appearing to six young children. She felt compelled to travel to Europe, across the entire world (at her own expense), in her search for **Truth**. She found it… or rather *Him*! She had a miraculous experience. When she returned, she was unrecognizable as my sister. Suddenly she had peace in her soul and a purpose to her life. She started to serve others and was no longer depressed and angry. Her change was so radical that my father took note and was dumbfounded. He started to read a lot about our Catholic Faith. Then, as the shepherd of our family, he began his new journey and, together with my mom, brought the rest of us closer to Christ in a personal way. I can assure you that without the experience my sister had in Medjugorje, I would not be writing this book today.

Who is Mary? Mary is a hero! She is a hero's hero. She is "the New Eve," one of God's greatest gifts to His children. She is the greatest spiritual warrior, the exemplification of humility, the intercessor, the Immaculate Conception, the Queen of Heaven and Earth... She is the Mother of GOD.

God refers to Mary, the "New Eve", directly after the fall of man. When denouncing Satan, the serpent, God states in Genesis 3:15 – "I will put enmity between you and the **woman**, and between your offspring and hers: He will strike at your head, while you strike at His heel."

God again speaks of Mary over seven hundred years *before* she was born in Isaiah 7:13-14:

> "Then he said: Listen O house of David! Is it not enough for you to weary men, must you also weary my God? Therefore the Lord Himself will give you this sign: the **virgin** shall be with child, and bear a son, and shall name him Immanuel."

God then describes this man in Isaiah 53:2-7:

> "There was in him no stately bearing to make us look at him, nor appearance that would attract us to him... Yet it was our infirmities that he bore, our sufferings that he endured, While we thought of him as stricken, as one smitten by God and afflicted. But he was *pierced* for our offenses, crushed for our sins, upon him was the chastisement that makes us whole; by his stripes we were healed. We had all gone astray like sheep, each following his own way; But the Lord laid upon him the guilt of us all. Though he was harshly treated, he submitted and opened not his mouth; *like a lamb led to the slaughter* or a sheep before the shearers, he was silent and opened not his mouth..."

God calls on Mary for the first time at the Annunciation: Luke 1:26-38:

"The Angel Gabriel was sent from God to a town of Galilee called Nazareth, to a virgin betrothed to a man named Joseph, of the house of David, and the virgin's name was Mary. And coming to her, he said, "Hail, favored one! The Lord is with you"... "Do not be afraid, Mary, for you have found favor with God. Behold, you will conceive in your womb and bear a son, and you shall name him Jesus. He will be great and will be called Son of the Most High, and the Lord God will give him the throne of David his father, and he will rule over the house of Jacob forever, and of his kingdom there will be no end." But Mary said to the Angel, "How can this be, since I have no relations with a man?" And the angel said to her in reply, "The Holy Spirit will come upon you, and the power of the Most High will overshadow you... Mary said, **"Behold, I am the handmaid of the Lord. May it be done to me according to your word."**

With that final statement, Mary did what Eve would not. She gave up herself to God. She gave up her control of her life. She gave up control of her future with her betrothed husband. She gave up her will and desire. She gave up her name which would be tarnished due to assumed sinful humiliation. She knowingly gave up her life, recognizing that the law of the land would have her stoned to death for being pregnant out of wedlock.

She did this all, defeating Satan at that moment who would have tempted her like Eve to "be like God" unto herself—to take control of her own life and destiny. Instead, through utter and complete humility, Mary allowed herself to be totally dependent on God. She allowed herself to be a child of God. She gave up control of everything including her fear, even though every instinct of her being was to shout out and say "no."

As all of mankind entered suffering and death through the actions of Eve, all of mankind is redeemed and can now enter eternal life through the actions of Mary. This is why she is referred to as the "New Eve."

She is also Satan's biggest nemesis. Satan was once the highest Archangel named Lucifer. He was the highest form of God's creation. It is in the incarnation of God, God becoming man (dust), that Lucifer, along with one third of the angels, chose to no longer be with God. He could not humble himself to serve man. Through his spite, his objective was, is, and forever will be, the pursuit of separating God's children from Him.

Satan is the tempter and the liar. Through the experience of my own weakness I can assure you that he is very good at his trade. That is, of course, until he met the likes of Mary. He had never been beaten by a human being. He can lose to Jesus, the Son of Man. However, he has a really hard time losing to Mary. It is through her humility that she personifies everything he is not. It is through her humility that God has elevated her to Queen of Heaven and Mother of God. As she stands firm in her humility, Satan can only "crawl on his belly" in "Eternal Fire" in rage and envy. After all, she only had to say 'no' to God and the Redeemer may never have been born.

As fantastically amazing as Mary is, she has no power of her own. Like the moon, she can only shed light on the world by reflecting the Son. She is always taking her children to Him. She is always there, lighting our path to Him.

What is clear is that Jesus listens to her. He followed the Ten Commandments and "honored his father and mother."(Ex20:12) One example of this was during the wedding feast at Cana. According to John 2:3-6, "When the wine ran short, the mother of Jesus said to him, 'they have no wine.' Jesus said to her, 'Woman, how does your concern affect me? My hour has not yet come.' His mother said to the servers, *'Do whatever He tells you.'*"

This story tells us a lot about the relationship between Christ and the "Woman." First, like God the Father in Genesis ("I will put enmity between you and the Woman"), Christ always refers to his mother throughout scripture as "Woman." Second, Christ obeyed his mother even though his hour "has not yet come," allowing her to intercede for the bride and groom. Finally, she instructed the servants to "do whatever He tells you."

This entire story is a microcosm of Mary's role in the universe. Mary intercedes for us. While raising nine kids, my mother's instinctual answer to the constant barrage of requests to her throughout a day was 'no.' That instinct of hers usually kept most of us out of trouble. We all knew that if we really wanted something, we could always pass the request through my father. He would intercede for us and, at times, the outcome would be quite different.

Mary intercedes for her children like this all of the time. There is no better person one could have whispering into the ear of the Lord than His mother. When Catholics recite the 'Hail Mary,' we are simply asking the Mother of God to intercede for us at the two most important times in our existence, "now and at the hour of our death." It is similar to asking your wife, cousin, mother, or friend to pray for you, like we all do when we are sick or facing challenges. The prayer to Mary has a bit more influence with our Lord however.

It would be foolish to "worship" Mary. Why would someone worship a creature other than God, especially if that creature had no power? Catholics do not worship Mary. Catholics honor her. If we want to be like Christ in all ways, we must honor His mother. This is especially true because He gave us His mother, His final gift from the cross, before His death.

During crucifixion, one would normally die through suffocation rather than by bleeding to death. This occurred because as one would hang on the cross, their arms would be stretched straight over their head and, over time, they would not be able to support their own body weight. In order for Christ to fully breathe, much less speak, He would have to pull on the nails holding His hands and push on the nail through His feet to elevate Himself on the cross in order to inhale enough in order to speak. In other words, it took a lot of effort and pain for Jesus to speak while He was hanging from the cross. It is because of this reality that I pay close attention to the few words of Christ while He was on the cross.

"When Jesus saw his mother and the disciple there whom he loved (John), he said to his mother, 'Woman, behold, your son.' Then he said to the disciple, 'Behold, your mother.'" John 19:26-27.

Jesus Himself gave us His mom to be our own. We all have this great mom who wants nothing more than for us to know her Son. She wants nothing more than for us to spend eternity with God and our eternal family in Heaven. I talk to Mary every day. I am a "mama's boy."

Jesus is not jealous of my love for her. It would certainly strain any relationship I would have with one of my friends if I brought him home to my house and he didn't honor, respect, or even want to talk to my mother. Jesus is the same. If I really want to love Christ; if I really want to know everything about Him; if I want to become one with Him; I need to know His mother.

Throughout time, Mary has appeared to visionaries in several places on Earth. In each one of these miraculous appearances, her message always points to her son saying "Do whatever He tells you." Before you shake your head and question the authenticity of these visions, you should know that the Catholic Church is the most skeptical party before declaring one of these visionary sites to be authentic. The Church launches full investigations which often take decades before declaring a miracle.

Many Catholic pilgrims flock to these sites where visions have occurred. These include Fatima Portugal, Lourdes France, Guadalupe Mexico, and Knock Ireland. The Church has yet to recognize Medjugorje because the visions are still occurring today and the investigation by the Church does not begin until the visions have ceased.

Following in the steps of my sister, many others in my family have since visited Medjugorje. Some have returned with more dramatic life changing stories than others. All have returned with a closer relationship to Christ from the experience. In going to Medjugorje, or making any pilgrimage for that matter, God seems to recognize our effort to know Him better. It is like in Scripture how the woman pushes her way through the crowd just to touch the hem of Jesus' cloak and was healed from her hemorrhaging. God seems to honor those who are willing to stop for a moment of their life and make a journey to see Him. He seems to respect those who have the faith that "if they were to only reach out and touch His cloak, they would be healed."(Mk 6:56)

When I think of Mary at the foot of the cross, I often try to put myself in her shoes. Can you imagine watching your child being beaten and tortured in front of you? Can you imagine the love of your life having a crown of thorns banged into his scalp, having nails driven through his hands and feet, and hung up like a criminal? Could you imagine a mother's instinct to simply want to hold her son who is suffering, wipe the blood from his face, and kiss him like she would have when he was a boy to make him feel better? As was foreseen by Simeon at Jesus' circumcision, her heart was truly pierced as she was tortured, sharing her son's pain. (Lk 2:34)

Better than anyone, Mary understands God's sacrifice for us. She is truly an example to all of us. In the end, I speak to Mary as first did the Angel Gabriel and Elizabeth (Mary's Aunt):

"Hail Mary, full of grace, the Lord is with thee. Blessed art thou among women and blessed is the fruit of thy womb, Jesus. Holy Mary, Mother of God, pray for us sinners now, and at the hour of our death. Amen."

SAINTS

I WORK A LOT WITH youth. I often hear from co-workers, "Look out for that troubled kid; he or she is a real handful." I take their advice and look out for them, but not because I think they could harm me. I look out for them as potential fantastic saints for God. These upstarts frequently have spirits that are bold and rebellious. These kids have a lot of energy and they are not afraid to use it.

I concluded that there is a lot of courage in rebellion. I know that the trick with these kids is to simply change what they are rebelling against. I convince them that their energy is great if used for the right purpose. If they could rebel against sin; if they can rebel against unhealthy cultural norms, they might end up being the greatest saints ever.

A saint is defined as anybody who is in Heaven. This includes all people who are with the Lord and it also includes the Angels. All the Saints and Angels are members of the "Body of Christ." Some of these members, by the authority bestowed upon the Catholic Church, have been declared Saints (what the church looses on earth is loosed in heaven, what is bound on earth is bound in heaven. Mt 16:5). Ironically, the Church with all of its authority has never damned an individual to Hell.

I would consider every *practicing* Catholic in today's society a rebel by default as our American cultural "norm" has deviated so far from Christian principles. Those who are Christian are now persecuted, ridiculed, and regarded as 'unenlightened.' Our media, public schools, colleges, and social elite have essentially labeled Christians as the enemy. This is not the first time we have been persecuted, nor will it be the last.

Jesus Christ Himself was a massive rebel. He was an upstart to man's perception of Truth and societal rule. He was such a rebel that the people "hung Him on a tree."(Acts5:30) I often note that I am probably not standing up for the Truth as boldly as I should, because I have yet to be martyred. With the way things are going, who knows? That day may not be as far off as I once imagined.

God never gives up hope for us. God has transformed some of the worst sinners into the greatest saints. For example, St. Paul literally hunted down Catholics and had them killed. He was not such a great guy until the Lord knocked him off his horse. Paul then redirected the energy he invested in finding and eliminating Christians to telling the world about Christ and the Truth.

St. Augustine, a Doctor of the Catholic Church, makes even teenagers of our generation look like a bunch of perfect saints by comparison. He simply directed the energy he spent on constant partying and sinful living to the new objective of knowing and loving the Lord. This was likely the result of his mother, Saint Monica, interceding for her son in prayer. She prayed for twenty years for his conversion of heart. Finally her prayers were answered. St. Augustine decided to come out of the darkness into the light. He eventually became a Bishop.

Some saints, however, have been saintly from the outset. St. Theresa, often called "The Little Flower," didn't ever seem to have had a dark, sinful time throughout her life. She died at a young age, but her simple writings were so profound that she is also honored with the title "Doctor of the Catholic Church."

The point is that **every human being, regardless of what they have done before, is called to be a saint now!** This is not some calling or expectation for everyone but me. This is not the call only for "holy people." This is God's expectation for me and for every person on Earth.

That Truth was hard for me to accept for a long time, but, in the end, I know that if I want to be in Heaven with God, this is my vocation: to be a saint. I have no higher calling in my life. As a husband and father, I have a responsibility to help my wife and children respond to their calling to that vocation as well. I remind my wife to pray. I teach my children to pray. Attending Mass is mandatory until they are old enough to move out. I educate my children about the Faith. God is the center of our family life. My wife has the burden of calling me to be better than I always want to be or think I could be…. Why do we do all this? Because I love them and they love me. I want them to get to Heaven. I hope to be with them all for eternity in the arms of our Lord. If they are not there, I will have failed in many ways.

I have encountered many saints in my life. They will likely never be officially recognized as saints by the Church, but they inspire me to holiness by their example and words. These people push me further than I would be inclined to push myself. They care about their eternal destiny. They love others unconditionally. They take the advice of St. Francis and "…preach all day and, if absolutely necessary, use words." Their lives are sermons. They rise above adversity and remain steadfast in their journey to eternal life with God.

As part of the "Body of Christ," the saints pray for us and with us. Like other members of our earthly family, we can ask them to pray for a special intention or ask for their help and intercession for us. Similar to our prayers to Mary, we do not pray to the saints like we pray to God. We do not worship the saints; they are not God. We talk to them as I am talking to you right now. They have no innate power. They can only advise us through their experience and can join with us and pray *with* us to God.

When there is an illness in the family or when I am going to take a big test, I ask my family to pray for me. The saints and angels in heaven are part of my family too. As a part of my family, they care about me and the decisions I make in my life. They are my biggest cheerleaders, rooting me on to make healthy choices.

Angels can physically and spiritually intervene in our lives. They are our protectors. We each have at least one guardian angel (Catechism of the Catholic Church: 336). We have all had moments in our lives when we have experienced unexplainable circumstances and have been spared suffering and death. For some reason in those situations the Lord utilized our angelic help to keep us around a bit longer. Obviously it was not yet our time. I pray that we learn to recognize God's intervention in our lives through our angels. How often I see people miraculously survive an illness or accident and shrug their shoulders, thanking "luck" for their life. During these occasions in my life when I have been spared, I pray that I have the grace to use the remaining time on this earth the Lord has given me to serve Him.

It is an amazing thought that when I am in Mass, the church is full of legions of angels, praising and glorifying God with me. Members of our family that have made it to heaven pray with us throughout the sacrifice of the Mass and become one with us during our reception of Holy Communion.

Saints are not people who never sin. Saints are people who have fallen to sin but keep getting up! They never give up. They do not allow themselves to forfeit to despair. They do not allow themselves to become apathetic to sin. They have hope in God's mercy and thus hope in their salvation. **Ultimately, every saint has a past and every sinner has a future**.

I pray that I might learn from those who have gone before me. I pray that, through God's grace, I can one day join my brothers and sisters in the arms of our Lord. I look forward to meeting all the people that influenced my opportunity to see God. I am excited to meet my angels. I thank God for the saints!

SUFFERING

REALITY: WE ARE ALL going to suffer at some point in our lives. The suffering may be physical, emotional, spiritual, or mental. As much as we try to avoid it, cover it up, or fear it, we will all suffer at some point. What a bummer.

I am not exactly an expert at suffering. The Lord has so far allowed me to live a pretty cushy life. I am not writing this chapter claiming I have somehow found a way to be impervious to suffering. Ask anybody who has seen me with the stomach flu; I am a pretty big wimp. That being said, in my short life the Lord has taught me a lot about suffering, although this is more through observation than experience.

First, it is through the consequences of the original sin of Adam and Eve that man brought death and all its related aspects into our world. God *allows* this consequence of sin to exist. As such, a significant amount of the suffering mankind endures is self-inflicted, either through the consequence of one's personal sins or through the sins of others.

Second, God chose to become *man* in the person of Jesus Christ. As a man, He willingly experienced and endured all forms of suffering and temptation that man experiences. He knows what we go through because He has gone through it Himself.

Third, although suffering is a reality that God allows, He uses suffering to benefit us in our journey with Him and to Him. It is this third point where the Lord has taught me the most.

One day I had an older couple in my office. In conversation, I quickly became aware that the woman had Alzheimer's disease. Her husband cared for her, loved her, and protected her. She didn't even know his name.

Later I asked the Lord, "Why do you allow Alzheimer's to exist? In essence the meaning of her life, the moment in time here on Earth for her to make the choice for God is over. Why would you continue to allow her to live?"

A short time after I asked the question, I was listening to Fr. Spitzer, President of Gonzaga University, speak on EWTN. The answer came through him in the form of the following story:

One day, 80 people were invited to a banquet. As they sat there, taking in the wonderful sights and aromas of their favorite food, they attempted to eat. Upon doing so, they discovered they were built without wrists and elbows. This realization caused wailing and gnashing of teeth as they were within inches of their favorite food, yet they could not feed themselves.

The first 20 people surmised, 'There must not be a God, because if there was, He would have built us with wrists and elbows.'

The second group of 20 replied, 'Well, the table is here, we are here, and we are not God, so He must exist. He must not be all powerful because if He was, He certainly would have made us with wrists and elbows.'

The third group of 20 stated 'God being God, He would be omnipotent; He would be all powerful. Therefore, He must not be a *loving* God if He created us without wrists and elbows.'

The fourth group of 20 looked at the others at the table in dismay, picked up their plates and leaned over the table to feed those across from themselves.

This fourth group of 20 realized they were built without wrists and elbows on purpose. They found they could never truly understand unconditional love if they only fed themselves throughout time. In sharing of themselves, in giving of their lives, in carrying that cross, only then could they experience sacrificial love: the deepest kind of love.

God allows Alzheimer's not for the spiritual benefit of the individual who has the disease. He allows the situation to exist to give the rest of us the chance to "feed her." In serving her, we receive grace and virtue, virtue that would otherwise be very difficult to obtain, virtue comprised of humility, patience, fortitude, compassion, wisdom, hope, and understanding. Serving her puts each person who encounters her into a spiritual 'boot camp' of sorts, molding the caregiver's soul and preparing it for eternal life with God. The woman's Alzheimer's illness may very well have saved her husband's soul and was therefore an eternal gift to him from God.

We will all suffer. Most of us will be cognitive through it. We will be acutely aware of our pain. This means that we will all have our chance to be like Jesus and carry a cross. He did not state, "I am carrying this cross so you don't have to carry one." Rather, Jesus challenges us to "Pick up *your* cross and follow me!" (Mt16:24) We will all have the chance to gain virtue through our suffering. We will all experience humility in allowing others to care for us.

It is interesting how we were created. We are born into the world as infants, totally dependent on others to care for us. We depend on our parents to feed us, clothe us, change our diapers, and keep us safe. We then grow into adults and often forget that "There is a God and I am not Him." We think we are God and mistakenly think we can control everything. We live life in utter pride. We then get older and our minds and bodies start falling apart. As we start losing our ability to move, hear, see, remember, eat, breathe, and ultimately wipe our own behind, we begin to quickly realize maybe we weren't God all along. Just maybe He was sustaining us this whole time! It is during this end of life experience when many find God for the first time through experiencing humility.

That is why euthanasia is so abhorred by the Church. It is through the crosses we all experience at the end of our lives and the associated growth of virtue that we, and those around us, inevitably grow spiritually. Many of us are then able to join God in Heaven. In many ways, we can suffer purgatory here on Earth. I am not saying we need to have a tug of war with God and stay alive at all costs. If someone has a terminal illness, there is nothing wrong with allowing nature to take its course. John Paul II did not choose to go back onto the ventilator at the end of his time here on Earth. Rather, he chose to die as naturally as possible and continue on his journey to join God in the afterlife.

The important issue I am addressing is the purposeful, intentional killing of someone, to "end their suffering." This killing includes the failure to maintain basic life support, such as food and water. Just as all healthy people will die if we were to turn the temperature of the hospital room up to 150 degrees, all healthy people will die without food and water. Cases in which feeding tubes are removed *and* sources of nutrition are withheld are murder (for example, the Terri Shiavo case).

We must instead serve those who are suffering. As the women served Christ on his journey with the cross, we are all called to serve each other when we are carrying our crosses. As in the case of the husband gaining in virtue for taking care of his wife with Alzheimer's, we too can grow in virtue when we serve one other. However, this does not mean that I have to *like* suffering; this does not mean I have to enjoy serving those who are suffering; this does not mean that I look for suffering; this does not mean that I do not fear suffering.

The good news is that I am in good company. Even Christ, during the agony in the garden the night before His death, asked God the Father to "Take this cup from me."(Mt 26:39) Like Christ, when I am suffering, I frequently ask the Father to ease my pain. Like Jesus, I also then pray that I have the strength and courage to state, "Thy will be done."

In being Catholic, I have found that the journey with Christ to the resurrection and eternal bliss must first include a journey with the cross. Being Catholic does not make me immune from suffering. If anything, the Lord is making me more and more aware of those who need to be fed, calling me to serve more and more people that I would have formerly overlooked as I am so frequently wrapped up in myself and my own needs.

If I know that I can use my crosses in life as Christ used His—for virtue for myself and grace for all mankind—then even in suffering I can still experience peace and joy. I remind myself that there are no such things as accidents. I have a choice at the moment of suffering: to wail and gnash my teeth, or to offer it up like Jesus for mercy and grace. I just think of the martyrs that were singing praise to God as they were burned alive or torn apart by the lions of the Coliseum. I think of St. Maximilian Kolbe who was joyful during his torture and death at a concentration camp during World War II. It is through the courageous and graceful acceptance of suffering by these martyrs that the observers of these events came to know God and were converted to Catholicism.

God puts all sorts of challenges in front of us on a daily basis. He gives us so many opportunities to choose Him. Most of the challenges and suffering I experience involves other people. What really helps me try to emulate Jesus, especially when I would otherwise try to run from the situation, is to look at the person I am trying to avoid as *Him.* An example of this would be at my workplace. I often have patients in the hospital that are cesspools of stench, secretions, fungus, and excoriated skin who are rotting from a cancer or who are not fully cleaned for a week after using the commode. Believe me, most of the time I would rather be anywhere else but there with that patient. I would rather get out of there for the sake of my comfort and find a way to distract myself in order to ignore their reality.

I then ask myself, "Would I run away from Christ as He was carrying His cross? Would I run from His filthy body as he was covered in blood and dust from repeatedly falling on His journey to His crucifixion? Would I run away from His bad breath and stench of blood and death? Would I be able to look upon his beaten face, bruised and covered in blood from His crown of thorns? Would I be willing to interrupt my day, even in the uncomfortable heat of Jerusalem, and help Christ with His cross on that journey?" If I remember to look at my patients as Him, I receive the grace I need to dive into the trenches of life.

I have a much harder time finding Christ in mean, annoying, or obnoxious people. Still, I have found that, with the right perspective, the Lord allows us to grow through the daily challenges of dealing with these people by growing in virtues such as compassion, patience, fortitude, judgment, and charity. I fondly call these people "Saint-makers" because without the crosses they have bestowed upon me, I don't believe I would be in the place the Lord desires me to be at this time. So, in essence, I have to thank the Lord for putting repulsive people into my life. I often wonder to whom I give crosses. I must "Saint-make" a lot. If you happen to be one of those people who have received the gift of my annoying behavior, know that I pray for you to have the patience to deal with me.

I have found that there are generally two reactions to bringing the light of Christ to people who are in a state of emotional, mental, and spiritual darkness. They will either see the light as it is and gravitate toward it, changing their life forever; or they are blinded by the light and lash out at the light blaspheming the Lord and all that is good. That is when I "shake the dust from my feet" (Mk16:11) and move on. Their *reaction* to the Truth is not my responsibility. My responsibility is to try to *be Jesus* to them, to choose at that moment to obey God's request of me. If they want to crucify me for that, so be it.

At the end of the day, I realize that I do not carry my crosses in vain. I also do not carry them alone. Jesus Himself helps me with my burden. It is He who "makes my burden light."(Mt11:30) As I carry my cross to the finish line, myriads of Angels and Saints are cheering me on. They intercede for me to have the strength. They pray that I will endure. I hope that one day, with their help, I will experience *my* resurrection. I yearn for the day when I can stand in front of God and hear from the Father, "Well done my good and faithful servant... welcome home!"

MISDIRECTED
COMPASSION

ONE DAY, ON A television show on EWTN, there was a priest in a room surrounded by several young people. These young adults were peppering the priest with question after question. The questions concerned the contemporary social "norms" about which the group thought the Church to be "out of touch." They questioned why the Church opposes gay marriage, homosexuality, contraception, extra-marital sex, abortion, woman being priests, stem cell research, euthanasia, in vitro fertilization, missing Mass, and boyfriend/girlfriend co-habitation before marriage. These questions were intermixed with their stated conclusion that the "Catholic Church has outdated views of society."

The priest stood there and absorbed what seemed like an eternity of questioning, almost like he was on the witness stand in a courtroom. The animated young people didn't seem to be interested in his initial answers to their questions. They continued asking the next question before he finished answering the prior question. He ultimately stopped responding to the verbal attacks, leaned back, and smiled. The commotion died down. Then the priest spoke.

"Has God Changed?" Bam! Then there was silence. These young adults got it. If God is Truth, the Truth does not change. God doesn't respond to opinion polls. The Truth doesn't change if a majority of people ignore it. The Truth doesn't change over time. *God* is the same today as He was yesterday and as He will be tomorrow. *Truth* is the same today as it was yesterday and as it will be tomorrow. Needless to say, no one in the crowd had any courage to ask him any more questions.

God is Truth. Meanwhile, Satan is referred to in scripture as the "Father of Lies."(Jn8:44) What he does is twist a person's desire to do virtuous acts and directs that effort to ultimately serve him and his perverted purposes. He is an expert in convincing us intellectually weak and unguarded humans to unwittingly join him in doing evil. One of his more subtle techniques is to take a person's natural feeling of compassion and misdirect it.

Our society unknowingly supports sin because we have *misdirected compassion*. We have compassion for the individuals called to self control and physical mastery. That is why we don't dare to encourage people to refrain from sex until marriage and until, as a married couple, they are open to life. We have compassion for the homosexual so we turn a blind eye to unnatural and sinful behavior. We have compassion for the woman who is choosing to terminate her child in an abortion. We have compassion for the couple who cannot conceive so we don't speak of the immorality of unnatural conception. We have compassion for the handicapped, so if the handicapped person is unborn, we 'compassionately' kill them through abortion. We have compassion for the physically ill, so we kill healthy unborn children for their cells to use in stem cell research. We have compassion for those who physically or mentally suffer, so we compassionately kill them (euthanasia). Boy, we sure kill a lot of people in the name of 'compassion.'

Our society is missing a major rule of basic morality. **The end does NOT justify the means!** In other words, even if we could cure humanity of the horrible disease of cancer by killing only one innocent, unwilling person, it is never moral to proceed. If our end is to reduce suffering by intentionally killing those who suffer, that is never moral. If we allow a woman to "pursue happiness," but in doing so she is massacring her children, that is never moral.

Many of our sins in this age are wrapped up in our desire to have unrestrained sex. If you think about it, if sex hurt there wouldn't be AIDS or STDs, children out of wedlock, abortion, or the need for contraception. There would literally be no infidelity.

I am not trying to claim that I am advocating that Catholics are to be prudes. On the contrary! God loves sex! Sex was the first commandment God gave to mankind. Once Eve was created, God commanded Adam and Eve to "Go forth and multiply!"(Gen1:22)

Sex has its proper place however. Marital love is an act of total self giving whereby I give myself to my spouse. It is pure and beautiful. Because it is an act where "two become one flesh," (Mt19:5) it clearly belongs in marriage. It requires eternal commitment. It is through this giving love between my wife and me that God allows our love to be manifested into new life. Children are walking, talking manifestations of the love shared between my wife and myself. It is through the giving love of two married people that God allows us to co-create with Him and thus create children made in His image. In giving of ourselves totally and completely, we accept each other's fertility, too. Otherwise, it would be like saying to my wife, "I love all things about you, Elizabeth, and I want you to share everything about yourself with me *except* your fertility." Marital love is a great gift from God. If I were to view marital sex with my wife as a "dirty" act, then I would be in as much error as someone who trivializes sex.

If sex is used to satisfy myself—my physical and emotional needs—and if the needs of my wife are secondary, then sex becomes a selfish act. If I was not married and I was having sex, I would be giving myself to another without commitment. This is again a selfish act. There is an emotional bond that occurs during sex whether we like it or not. If I were to have numerous sexual partners before marriage, then by continually breaking that bond with others I would be essentially practicing for divorce. I would be fearful of fully giving myself to anyone and I would be fearful of commitment because, in the end, I would be programmed with the belief that commitment is temporary. I wouldn't fully give myself to another because, with a history of repeatedly breaking up, I would want to avoid the anticipated pain of separation. After living a life of sexual encounters without commitment, I would gradually lose my ability to sustain a trusting relationship. This attitude would follow me into marriage, leading to a deep sense of loneliness. My marriage would always be on the brink of divorce.

Before I was married, if I were to give myself to others in sex, it would be totally disrespectful to my future bride. I would instead want to be able to give myself purely to her, without any baggage. I have never heard of a serious couple in a relationship say, "Boy, I am glad you slept around before we were married." After all, my body isn't only mine to give away. My body is my wife's and God's. I am simply the steward. I try to remain in good health and physical form for my wife because I love her. I also remain physically healthy because I respect the vessel that God chose to give me that houses the only thing that is truly mine: my soul, my will. If I were to use my body to cause lust in others, if I were to use my body to elevate myself, I would yet again forget that "There is a God and I am not Him" and practice the religion of individualism. **Extramarital sex is always an affront to a lasting, healthy, marital relationship.**

Self-giving love, however, produces life. As I mentioned before, if I were to perform the marital act and not be open to life, I would not be giving myself totally and completely to my wife and therefore that act would be selfish. That does not mean that I must *try* to have a baby every time my wife and I intimately celebrate marriage. Being Catholic does not necessarily mean we are all called to have 10 kids. However, we must be *open to life*. God gave us the natural monthly cycle of the woman. If spacing children is absolutely necessary for serious reasons economically or physically, we can abstain from sex on those days most likely to end in conception. Having children takes discernment about whether my wife and I can properly raise that child in body, mind, and soul. This discernment also requires prayer: What does God desire? What is His will? Have I truly given God and my spouse all of myself, including my fertility?

I once asked a priest, "what are the differences between 'Natural Family Planning' and contraception?" He responded that in "Natural Family Planning," the marital act itself is unchanged. Nothing is withheld. Natural Family Planning is not contraception. Each spouse still gives fully to each other without pills, coverings, gels, or other barriers. The very same monthly cycle by the woman and the marital act are also used when one is *trying* to conceive. The woman's monthly cycle is God's design, not ours. It fosters communication between spouses. It requires patience and self control. Natural Family Planning fosters self giving love. It allows each spouse to accept each other fully and respect one another's fertility, appreciating that aspect which makes each of us distinctly male or female.

In short, sex is meant to be unitive and procreative. We cannot and should not separate the two. If I were to conceive without the marital act by resorting to in vitro fertilization or the use of a surrogate donor, no unitive act has been performed and it is therefore unhealthy spiritual behavior. This is not to mention that even in the act of fertilizing eggs in a Petri dish, numerous new human beings are created and many are discarded. Then to compound the moral problem, the practitioners try to increase the odds of achieving pregnancy by implanting numerous fertilized eggs into the uterus. As several children eventually begin to grow, the couple will ultimately "selectively terminate" some of their own children. Children are a gift from God, not a right. Although it is an extremely difficult cross to bear, infertile couples are called to consider adoption as an alternative. That would be the healthy spiritual choice for those couples.

If I were to use sex only for the unitive aspect and I wasn't open to life, then I would also be engaging in unhealthy spiritual behavior. That is one of the many reasons why contraception and homosexuality are not condoned by the Church.

Homosexuality is a sexual disorder among numerous other sexual disorders. These include pedophilia, sadomasochism, and exhibitionism. If homosexuality was not disordered and was the natural order of our creation, would our species continue to exist?

There has been a claim that homosexuals are "born that way." Many in our society often question how Catholic teaching can be so "closed minded" by not permitting the homosexual to act on their sexual urges. This is an invalid argument. Pedophiles may be born with their sexual disorder also. We do not encourage *them* to act upon their sexual urges. Exhibitionists may be born with their sexual disorder, we do not encourage them to run into Giants Stadium naked and show themselves. What is the difference between these disorders and homosexuality?

Some argue that homosexuality would not seem disordered if we were to stand in the shoes of the homosexual. I would then argue that pedophilia is not disordered to the pedophile. Exhibitionism is not disordered to the exhibitionist. In fact, *if we were to look through the eyes of the disordered on any issue, there would be no such thing as disorder.*

It is not a sin *to be* a homosexual! It is a sin to *act upon* those disordered instincts. My problem with the homosexual revolution in this country is that it is a *celebration of disorder.* We are trying to integrate and "naturalize" a lifestyle and behavior that is clearly unnatural.

The homosexual revolution is trying to equate the sinful, spiritually destructive act of homosexual contact with the holy, beautiful, life-giving union between a man and woman in marriage. The Father of Lies has outdone himself in getting unsuspecting accomplices to support this contemporary movement. His perverted concept undermines the family, the building block of a healthy society. It contributes to the trivialization of sex in our nation. It is unclear whether the trivialization of sexual love occurring between heterosexuals is promoting homosexuality or vice versa. In either case, the end result is that we are distorting a profoundly great gift from God.

Catholics are called not to just be charitable to homosexuals. **We are called to love them.** We are called to love them as if they were Jesus Christ to us. This means we are certainly not called to mock them, injure them, persecute them, or discriminate against them in terms of employment or housing or anything. Who would Jesus eat with and minister to in today's society? After all, it was He who challenged the crowd, "He who has no sin, cast the first stone." However, we must never forget that Jesus then turned to the woman who had performed adultery and stated, "Go and sin no more."

"Tolerance" of sin and evil has never been, nor should ever be, a Catholic virtue. Catholics are called to practice *charity* *to those in sin.* In the end, we are all sinners (especially me.) We all have weaknesses. We all have crosses to carry. I have compassion for everyone in their weakness (including homosexuals.) That does not mean that I want to ever condone or even be apathetic to sin.

The reason why sin and evil are flourishing in our society is <u>not</u> because evil has somehow become stronger than it used to be. **It is through the apathy about sin by good people that sin has taken a stronghold in today's world.** Satan has caused good people to become confused. He often convinces good, holy people to avoid standing up for the Truth for fear of being hypocrites. Through this fear, Satan then acts in our society unopposed. Society then tolerates a moral code which is based upon the least common denominator of human decency.

The truth is: **we are all hypocrites!** The only non-hypocrites that have ever walked the earth are Jesus Christ and the Virgin Mary. Just because we are sinners does not mean that we should not strive to be better in mind and deed. Just because we are weak, we should not lower the "moral bar" of our society to our present state of weakness.

Likewise, we are admonished by the "politically correct" proponents, "Do not judge others!" It is true that we should not judge whether others are going to Hell. Rather, we should have mercy on all who are in error and encourage them to "sin no more." However, Satan has twisted our thinking about judging *people's souls* (predicting whether they are going to heaven or hell) versus judging an *action* as good or evil.

The result of this twisted thinking and rampant confusion is that the discernment between good and evil has become a social taboo. The Truth is: **we must judge *actions* as good or evil.** If we are aware that an action is evil and sinful due to the teaching and example of Christ, then we know it is damaging to the soul. It is like a spiritual cancer. If we love others in our society, we have a responsibility to educate them on the difference between healthy behavior and unhealthy behavior. If we know the stove is hot, we must tell others before they touch it. We cannot sit idly by and allow sin to become our cultural 'norm.' In this case, to do nothing—to be apathetic—is to sin!

Stand up! Stand up for the Truth! Stand up for all that is good! Be a light in this time of darkness! Stand up for our Lord! Stand up for our Master! Stand up for our King!

LIFE

SHE IS IN THE eighth grade. She looks like an angel from heaven. In her early childhood she had blond ringlets that would have made Shirley Temple jealous. She has almond brown eyes that are the doorway to her soul. She enjoys boys and her circle of girlfriends. She gets straight A's in school (quietly) and is mature beyond her years. She loves to paint and draw. She enjoys softball and surfing. She loves her dog and her parents. She would say she has had a great life. She has dreams of her future and has ambition and goals. She is loved by all who encounter her. She is the kind of young lady that would seek out and befriend the new kid in class, not because she lacked friends, but because it is her nature. She is the joy of so many that have had the privilege to know her. Some day she will make a man very happy in marriage. They will have children of their own and grandchildren and great-grandchildren. It is through this life of hers that generations of lives will inherit such goodness, such peace and love. This great life, this fantastic person was a hairs-breadth from an early death.

Life simply cannot be imagined if she were not here. All who have encountered this young lady would not have experienced how bright and wonderful this life on Earth can be if she was not a part of it.

Meanwhile, the mother-to-be of this young lady grew up in a culture which bombarded her with values contrary to Catholic teaching. As her own value system formed, she did come to believe that sexual intimacy was to be reserved until you found someone "you love." However, there was never an expectation of holding onto that gift

81

until reaching the commitment of marriage. As a result, at age 16, this teenager gave herself for the first time to her boyfriend of several years. She happened to be fertile and thus became pregnant.

When she first became aware of her situation, she told her boyfriend and his parents. They immediately went into a state of denial. They simply refused to accept that reality. They just hoped the situation would disappear. They wouldn't allow their son to speak to her or associate with her in any way. The boyfriend's parents and her boyfriend abandoned her in her time of need.

Meanwhile, something had to be done. There was the obvious problem: this 16 year-old, pregnant teenager was afraid to tell her parents. She was fearful that they would never understand. What if they rejected her also? What if they kicked her out of the house? She felt all alone, completely alone.

Desperate thoughts filled her mind. She knew there was a way out. All she had to do was have an abortion. No one would know. It would solve all of her problems. She could continue life like nothing had happened.

Then God intervened. Grace abounded. Truth kissed her. Suddenly she was enlightened and saw the problem clearly. If she had an abortion, *she* would know; *God* would know. She could never escape herself. She would never be able to face herself. Her maternal instinct screamed to her that if she were to destroy the child inside her, she would be destroying a part of her own soul.

She waited until her father was not around before she told her mother. She felt her mother would be more understanding than her father. Good news. Her mother was supportive. Together they decided to tell her father when he was away on business and thousands of miles away from home. Distance would be a protective buffer.

They called her father. Much to their surprise, there was no explosion. There were no threats. The father immediately began to help. Inspired by the Spirit, he contacted his married brother. His brother and his brother's wife had wanted children for years but could not have them naturally. This was an answer to their prayers!

The pregnant teenager was invited to live with her aunt and uncle during the ensuing months. Finally the teenage mother gave birth to her beautiful, baby girl who was then immediately adopted by the mother's aunt and uncle. It is through this "bad" situation that tremendous goodness was released into the world. This young teenage girl gave her aunt and uncle the love of their lives. The child has, and hopefully will continue to have, a great life. The teenage mother faced adversity and, with God's grace, triumphed. In delivering that child, the teenage mother for the first time in her life realized that God is *real*! In carrying her cross, she *experienced* God's love for her. She died to herself and became resurrected into a woman of honor, character, dignity, and strength. In her fall, with her determination to get back up, she understood her call to be a saint. She was being molded by God for her true love in her marriage to come. She was being prepared for her soul-mate. She was being prepared to become *my wife*. There are no accidents.

The fateful day my wife chose to allow her child to live, over 4,000 women in the United States faced that same decision and made a tragic mistake. Undoubtedly most of these women are good people, perhaps even holy people. But in their moment of distress, in their moment of abandonment, they are "helped" by parents, doctors, and friends who have bought into the biggest lie of our age. These misguided helpers with their misdirected compassion, these unwitting accomplices to the "Father of Lies", convince these young pregnant women to abort their own babies. After all, they argue, it is the "right" of the mother to terminate her pregnancy. The unborn baby has no rights. The unborn baby has not yet achieved 'personhood'; the unborn baby is really only a fetus. It is only a very small, unimportant glob of tissue.

We must all seek the Truth in this issue. Too much is at stake to put our heads in the sand and pretend that there is not a problem. It helps if we realize that "there is a God and I am not Him." It helps if we are willing to spend a few minutes and reflect with openness. Think about it. Society must acknowledge that the unborn are genetically human. Human women do not deliver dogs or elephants or carrots or fish. Society must also agree that the unborn entity is "alive." Unborn people, like born people, are composed of cells that are growing, reproducing, metabolizing, and living.

Our society and justice system made a law in Roe vs. Wade that doesn't allow that unborn, human, alive, child to achieve '*personhood*' until the unborn child has fully passed through some invisible magical force-field in the birth canal. Without personhood, even though the unborn child is alive and human, the unborn child is not protected under our laws.

It is therefore fully legal to experiment on the child or use that child's nervous system as spare parts for the handicapped in "embryonic stem cell research." It is also fully legal to burn the skin off of this unborn child with chemicals until they bleed to death, dismember this child by sharp surgical instruments, and eviscerate this child through high powered suction and blending. It is even legal during delivery to stab a partially born child in the back of the skull and remove the child's brains while the child is still in the birth canal. This "partial birth abortion" is legal as long as a portion of the child's body remains in the mother. Five seconds later, when the child is completely outside the birth canal, stabbing the child is considered murder. *Have we completely lost our minds?*

Legal abortion is not the first time that genocide was justified by denying the personhood of alive, human beings. Hitler justified the Holocaust because the Jews were not classified as 'persons' under German law. Our United States Supreme Court justified slavery through the "Dred Scott Decision" whereby African-Americans were not given 'personhood' and were therefore enslaved like livestock. There has never been a time in human history when mankind has been right when separating the status of 'personhood' from alive, human beings.

That is why the Catholic Church, long before our Declaration of Independence, identified all human beings as having the inalienable rights of "life, liberty, and the pursuit of happiness." Inalienable rights are rights that we don't have to earn. They are rights that are inherent to us because we *exist* and because of our respect for human life and human dignity. The most basic of these rights is the *right to life* because, without it, all other rights are irrelevant. If you are dead, your other rights are of little value.

Ironically, the 'personhood' of the child in modern culture is based solely on whether or not the mother *wants* the child to be a person. The unborn child is protected under the laws *if* the mother wants to 'keep her baby.' For example, if a pregnant woman is murdered, the murderer gets charged with two counts of murder. What is unbelievable about this is that the mother can, at any time, go and kill that child in an abortion and our society will subsidize that abortion through Planned Parenthood. Does this make any sense to anybody?

If a mother looks at her child and decides that she does not want her child to be a person anymore, does that child objectively cease to be a child? If that same woman looked at a tree and declared that it was not a tree, does the tree objectively cease to be a tree? Why do different principles apply to the unborn?

At what stage of development does the unborn child become a person? The pro-abortionist would argue that at any time during the nine months before birth the unborn child "has not yet developed into a human-being." They would claim that in the first few weeks and months of life the unborn child is "just a few cells."

My retort is that that child is *supposed* to be a few cells at that age. I have five children. My 2 week old doesn't look like my one-year-old who doesn't look like my four-year-old who doesn't look like my seven-year-old who doesn't look like my nine-year-old. They are all still developing and will be until death. This development started at conception. It did not begin after they passed through the magical, invisible force field in the birth canal. A one-day-old, unborn, one-celled child is supposed to go through that normal stage of human development. This logic is also true of a more developed three-week-old unborn child and an even more developed eight-month-old. That is normal human development. Everyone reading this chapter was once a one-celled unborn child that continued growing before and after birth. In short, the act of birth did not cause development to cease. Therefore, the argument that the child isn't "developed" is not applicable.

If 'personhood' is to be assigned at some random moment of development, what happened in that moment of time that justifies that conclusion? For example, if 'the line' is at 3 months for the unborn, is the child truly not the same at 2 months, 29 days, 23hrs and 59 minutes? Of course the child is the same! The moment is arbitrary. If you were to ask, "What is the difference in a child as we go back in time, second by second?" the answer is the same. Nothing! You would find yourself having to start at conception to assign the title of personhood.

Some argue for abortion by saying that the child might be "born into a poor environment." If abortion is compassionate for the poor, why discriminate? The same principle should be applied to all the poor and we should then be 'compassionately' eliminating everybody we consider to be poor.

Some argue that the child might be handicapped. If that is the principle, we should consider 'compassionately' killing all those who have handicaps now. In short, for whatever 'compassionate' reason abortion is justified, the same principle should then apply to those of us fortunate enough to have passed through the magical, invisible force-field of the birth canal.

Every time my wife is pregnant, we hear the comment from good hearted people: "as long as the baby is healthy..." I have always thought to myself, "and if they are not?" There are no guarantees in life. My children might get into a car accident or become ill at any time. Would I be expected to abort them then?

Some people are confused because abortion has been made legal. They have unwittingly fallen into the moral trap that "since an act is legal, it is therefore moral." If our great democracy voted to make rape legal, would it then be moral? Should we not have a law against rape, even if some are going to break the law and rape women anyway?

Many focus on the 7% of abortions done for medical reasons or rape and incest and therefore turn a blind eye to the other 93% of abortions done strictly with the mindset of birth control.

In regards to rape and incest, abortions done for these reasons are about 1%. Studies have proven that when a woman has an abortion after a rape, she still suffers from post-abortion syndrome. In many ways, having that abortion is like allowing that rapist to control her again. The child also didn't ask to be there. If the child of the rapist was born and standing in front of us, could we justify killing the child then? There are many families that would be more than willing to adopt that child and, in a way, the mother of that child could live the rest of her life knowing the rapist didn't turn *her* into a murderer. In the end she defeated evil and turned a negative situation into a positive one.

Consider the mother that has an abortion for medical reasons. The Catholic Church is clear in this situation. If the mother's *life* is in jeopardy during a pregnancy, *her* life is not less valuable than the life of her child. The effort should then to be to save *both* the mother and child, even if that means delivering the child early and doing our best to save that child. This approach holds even if the odds of rescue are slim. We should still give the child a chance at pulling through. If there was an avalanche that buried skiers, we would still search for them even if the odds of survival are low and the path treacherous. If the mother had cancer and needed chemotherapy which would be harmful to the unborn child, it would still be permissible as her intention would be to treat the cancer, not to harm her child.

The same reasoning applies to the treatment of an ectopic pregnancy. An ectopic pregnancy is the situation whereby an unborn child implants somewhere other than uterus, often in the fallopian tube. If that portion of the fallopian tube is not removed, *both* mother and child would die. Removal of that portion of the fallopian tube is essential to prevent the same situation from occurring again. The *intention* is never to kill the child although that is the inevitable outcome. The intention should be to save the lives of both, in all circumstances, if possible. *Intention is everything.*

Pay attention to our politicians as they discuss this however. The pro-abortionists don't discuss the *'life'* of the mother; they discuss the *'health'* of the mother. Health has been defined by the Supreme Court in Doe vs. Bolton as "mental, psychological, emotional, or financial health." **Abortion is legal until *birth* in all states of this country if the mothers 'health' is in question**. In other words, at nine months gestation, at which time the mother could have a c-section, she can legally abort her child if she states that she is depressed or not financially 'healthy.'

In embryonic stem cell research, our country has compassion for those who are ill or handicapped. Through that 'misdirected compassion,' we are legalizing experimentation on the unborn and the use of their parts. What I would like answered by Michael J. Fox and his followers is the question: "How many children are you willing to slaughter for their parts so you don't have Parkinson's disease anymore? 1,000? 100? 10? 1?" Again, are we going to allow the ends to justify the means?

Some argue that this is a private issue and the government should stay out of it. If that same child was born and lived in the privacy of the woman's home, and the woman was burning off her child's skin or stabbing the back of the child's skull with a scissors, wouldn't the child's right to life supersede that woman's right to privacy?

What does this mean? The Truth of this matter is hard to comprehend. More children are killed every single day in this country than were killed on the 9/11/2001 Twin Tower attack in New York City. More children are killed in our country *each year* than have died in all wars America has ever fought. Nearly every third child conceived is aborted. More than 50,000,000 lives have been slaughtered in this contemporary American Holocaust. Why?

It all comes down to the most predominant "religion" in the United States today: *the Religion of Individualism.* Abortion is just a symptom of the mindset of our time. We want to live a life without consequence. This includes, of course, our sexual life. We want to have 'the freedom' to have sex with anything that breathes and not have to worry about consequences. Again, children are a perceived threat for the quest of power and control. Children are now perceived by many as a burden. Our society therefore continues to ignore the blatant Truth and the magnitude of the abortion problem.

Instead of cherishing our women and honoring them in their femininity and supporting them when they are pregnant, with abortion we destroy that which distinguishes women from men. We attack every fiber of maternal instinct and minimize the human life growing inside of her as "just a blob of cells." In essence, we are all just a blob of cells. Abortion and embryonic stem cell research are evil. **Abortion and embryonic stem cell research are acts that are *always* rooted in selfishness.** They are wrong, every time, always… period. The Catholic Church defines abortion as "gravely immoral."(CCC 2272) In participating in an abortion, whether having one, advising friends or family to have an abortion, promoting the abortion cause, or intentionally voting for politicians who advance abortion in our society, one is placing on oneself a "lampshade of sin" thick enough to block out the light, that is, the life of grace given to us. We become separated from God.

As was mentioned, one third of pregnancies end in abortion. *Think* of how many people you know who may have had an abortion. Think of how many boyfriends and fathers and parents and friends were instrumental in encouraging that act. Perhaps one of the reasons why abortion still exists in this country is that there is a subconscious, mistaken belief that since "everyone is doing it," and we live in a democracy, we are safe from personal responsibility and the judgment of God. To correct the error it would take countless people to practice humility and have the capacity to admit making a massive mistake.

Most find it simply easier to pretend nothing is wrong. It would seem that many are afraid of having participated in this level of evil, and therefore feel the urge to fight to keep the lie alive. It would be like being a German who sought out Jews to send to a concentration camp or working in the concentration camp itself and deciding later that Jews are people too. It takes a lot of courage to become self-aware.

For those who have participated in abortion, welcome to the 'sinners club.' God is merciful. The light of God in all of our lives is always on, waiting for us to repent and remove the "lampshades" we have placed over His light. In repentance and humility, we have the ability to allow the grace of the cross of Christ back in our lives and we can once again be set free of this great burden of sin. Jane Roe (from Roe v. Wade), whose real name is Norma McCorvey, understood this and repented. She became aware of how she was "used" by those with misdirected compassion to further their cause. That is why she became a Christian and is now a leader in the fight to end abortion. She is a hero and is now working on sainthood. She is on the path that can lead to eternity with God. Finding this path and staying on it is the goal of every saint. Every saint has entered this path at a different point in his or her life, usually found through humility and repentance.

What now? I had to first accept the gravity of the present situation, especially politically. Does it really matter if I have a perfect candidate in every other issue such as gun control, taxes, education, health care, and national defense if that candidate is for the slaughter of 4,000 children each day? Does the importance of any other issue come remotely close? Readers, please consider making the end of abortion a top priority by voting for the candidate that is most pro-life, whether that candidate is a Republican, a Democrat, or an Independent.

Secondly, use your voice. Speak for the unborn as they cannot speak for themselves. Talk to anyone who will listen. Encourage uniting those looking to abort their children with the thousands upon thousands of couples flying all over the world to adopt a child because there are so few children left here at home to adopt.

Thirdly, pray. After that, pray some more. Pray for a conversion of hearts. Pray for an end to the Religion of Individualism. Pray for awareness to the Truth. Pray for God to have mercy. Become a light in this time of darkness.

The good news is that, like the end of slavery and the end of the Jewish Holocaust, mankind ultimately comes to its senses. The question is: how many millions of children will be slaughtered in the interim? How many souls of the living will die spiritually as a result of this atrocity? And the final question we should ask ourselves: *will I be able to look at my grandchildren in the eyes and state that I did everything in my power to stop this bloodshed?*

CAMP VERITAS

THERE HAS ALWAYS BEEN an undercurrent of spiritual preparation and learning occurring throughout my whole life. As I entered my teen years and grew in my relationship with the Lord, I became more aware of this reality. Since then I have tried to allow the Holy Spirit to take control of my everyday life and, in doing that, I am now convinced that **there are no accidents**. Therefore, I try to learn from every situation, whether I perceive it as good or bad, and try to identify and understand what God is trying to teach me.

The Lord is merciful. He usually only shows me the next few steps of the journey. It is like climbing a mountain in the fog. If I truly saw how large and treacherous the mountain was before I started, I probably would not have bothered trying to climb it, telling the Lord His expectations of me were impossible.

The good news is that I don't see the whole mountain; I see only the next several yards and they don't look that difficult. With that limited visibility, I find myself often doing what I would have formerly considered for me to be unlikely. For example, if my English teachers in high school were told then that I would one day be writing a book, they would have laughed out loud.

There have been many learning situations in which the Lord has taught me profound lessons. One of these lessons occurred at a point in my life when I was having a difficult time at work. I was trying to control a situation to help make our business more successful. The problem was that I was not the 'top dog' where I worked and my warnings and suggestions were not always heeded. Following a tense meeting with my employers, I was totally stressed out. I started obsessively planning my next move: who I would talk to, what I would I say, and when would I say it. As usual, when my mind got into that obsessive problem solving mode, I shut out everything else. I was distant to my family. I didn't sleep well. I was unable to focus on normal tasks at hand.

It was during this stressful time that my wife recommended that I attend daily Mass with her. I agreed. Upon arrival, we chose to sit in a front pew of church. Following Mass, a woman I had never met before approached me. I found out later that she is a Jewish convert to Catholicism. She said, "The Lord wants me to tell you something." I thought to myself, "Yeah, right lady," but I listened just to be polite. She continued, "The Lord wants you to know that He really loves you. He has great plans for you. Don't worry about it; He will take care of it." With those words, she gave me a hug and walked off.

Instantly the flood of thoughts turning the treadmill in my brain stopped. I could no longer even *think* about my work-related petty worries. I felt mental and emotional peace. Her statement became the motto of my life: **If the Lord loves me, what else really matters?** Everything else is anxiety about the false control I *think* I have when I forget that **there is a God and I am not Him**. If I can look at that cross and truly believe God loves me, nothing else matters. My only remaining task is to fulfill the meaning of my life and choose to obey the Lord, moment by moment, in my life. That inclination to obey flows from having the faith that the Lord knows what He is doing.

After this episode of enlightenment, I continued to listen to the Lord and my next step up the mountain of life began to emerge from the fog. The Lord made me acutely aware of the condition of the Catholic Church in the Northeastern region of the United States. It is dying! The mean age of the community is rising. The youth are not retained following their Confirmation in eighth grade. The number of men answering the call to priesthood is dwindling. It is only a matter of time before churches are closed. Many churches will disappear, not in a hundred years or fifty years, but in the next twenty years unless something changes. The "religion of individualism" permeates deeply within the contemporary thinking of our culture.

These inspired thoughts from the Lord kindled a fire in me. I suddenly felt the need to stop *talking* about the problem and start *acting* on the solution. The next step was to focus on the youth. They **must** be filled with a spiritual fire. The approach to be taken was revealed: stamp out the religion of individualism; introduce them to their God; and let them experience God's love for them.

But how was this to be done? God had the answer, of course. His idea: Camp Veritas (veritas in Latin means "truth"). Camp Veritas would be an overnight camp where the youth of the Faith stop the business of their lives for a week and go to an earthly "heaven" to be with the Lord. The camp would offer education about the Faith, teach the kids how to pray, fill them with grace through Confession and the reception of the Eucharist, and introduce them to a vibrant community of believers, including priests and other religious. This religious experience would be provided in the setting of an outdoor camp with standard camp activities. In short, the objective of the week would be to "play and pray" and activate in each young Catholic camper the following desire: to reevaluate their life priorities by questioning where they came from and where they are going, and continue *in the Lord* one step at a time up the mountain of life.

My initial approach was to propose the idea to the staff of the Archdiocese of New York. The response I got from them was essentially, "Great, we'll pray for YOU in this mission!" My reaction was human and typical. I thought they didn't understand that I was trying to have them focus *their* resources on the youth in this venture. But I wasn't going to give up easily. The next step was to send another letter, only this time directly to Cardinal Egan—the man at the top—reiterating the concept of Camp Veritas more clearly and forcefully. Much to my disappointment, the response from him was essentially the same. This time, Cardinal Egan himself wrote me a letter again essentially stating, "Good luck. I will pray for YOU." Okay God, now what?

I prayed about this one for a long time. What on Earth did I know about teaching the youth, much less starting a camp or running a camp? In my medical profession I did not have regular interaction with the youth. Of course I was open to having a lot of my own children and raising them, but I had never been led before to get actively involved with other young people.

Also, it quickly became apparent to me that starting a camp would entail a lot of time and money. It would detract from my family responsibilities. In reference to this scenario, St. Paul stated it accurately, "It is better to be single, only proceed with marriage if you must."(1Cor7:27) I did not understand that statement until I got married. Before I was married, the Lord would say "jump" and I would ask "how high?" Since marriage, the Lord says "jump" and I turn to my wife and ask, "Honey, how high are *we* going to jump?"

The good news is that my wife has the same priorities in her life that I have in mine. Our priority is Heaven. It is through this reality that she feels called to "hold down the fort". Her attitude allows me to then "go forth." I have been truly blessed to have a wife that understands the big picture; she is like the supply train to the battlefield for souls.

The Lord was showing me the first few steps of the "mountain in the fog," so I started climbing. After all, if *I* do not act, who will? I started this climb up this mountain with the foundation of who I am; I began by presenting the idea of Camp Veritas to my immediate family. After all, they are the most Catholic people I know. These are God's saints. My family is full of holy, talented, and intelligent people who love the Church. They are not blind to the bleak future of the Church in our region… if nothing changes.

The reaction I received from those I love most was surprising. My parents and most of my siblings shook their heads, laughed, and told me that an idea of this magnitude could not be done. I was told the project was "unrealistic" and the problems we face in our Church were simply "too big."

My older brother, who has been a great example of faith to me in my life, relayed his personal experience with trying to renew our Faith. A year earlier he tried to start a city-wide youth prayer group. He invited hundreds of young adults to his parish for their opening meeting. Flyers were placed at numerous local parishes to invite young people. My brother asked his parish priest to order fifteen pizzas for the crowd he was expecting. To his dismay, his priest ordered three pizzas and told my brother he would order more if needed. Needless to say, the wise priest was correct in his expectations. Only three people showed up. Those three people were my brother, and two of his siblings. My brother's conclusion was that the Church was already dead in our region and beyond life-support.

My older sister (whose conversion was the catalyst for my family's conversion in the Faith, who attends daily mass and home-schools her seven saintly children) did not believe teenagers would ever willingly attend this camp, much less convince their parents to pay a fee for them to attend. She brought up the numerous logistical challenges I would face in opening a camp, such as adult volunteer supervision, the need for lifeguards, entertainment, and so forth. As she spoke, the magnitude of this task the Lord had placed in front of me was unveiled. This mountain was enormous. The journey ahead seemed so hard, so impossible. Looking back, that moment reminds me of Peter trying to convince Jesus not to enter Jerusalem where He would be crucified. The Gospel of Mark describes His response. "At this He turned around and, looking at His disciples, rebuked Peter and said, 'Get behind Me Satan. You are thinking not as God does, but as human beings do.'"(Mk8:33)

My younger sister, who was just brought back from the fringe of spiritual death through bulimia, is one of the most holy people I know. She spends over an hour each day in Eucharistic Adoration. Not only did she think the idea of this Camp was too big; she especially thought the idea was too big for me. The problem I was facing with my family is that they know me best. They know of my many weaknesses. They know the road I have traveled. She had no faith in *me*. What she didn't realize is that I do not have faith in *me* either. I am nothing in the grand scheme of things. Who am I to even attempt something as crazy as Camp Veritas? She believed I was having delusions of grandeur. Although I don't believe I am a prophet, it reminds me of Jesus saying, "Amen, I say to you, no prophet is accepted in his own native place."(Lk4:24) My immediate family members, who are very holy and very religious, did not believe in this idea. It did not take a genius to imagine what the entirety of the Catholic Church family might think, considering the deteriorating state of affairs.

Ironically, the only person in my immediate family who thought the idea of Camp Veritas had any value, and who didn't shoot the idea down outright, was my youngest sister (the same sister who finally attended Mass after the fly repeated landed on her face). Go figure?

The truth is that my family was right. All their objections and concerns were completely valid. I did not have any answers for them. In fact, I agreed with all their objections. I thought the Lord was crazy for asking me to start a camp. But that was the point. The only thing I really knew for certain was that the Lord was asking me to do this. I had faith in that call of the heart. I had faith without understanding. Although I felt completely alone at that moment—although the mountain looked too big for me to climb—the only response I could give to my family was, "I told the Lord I would try to answer His call and that I would give my absolute best, so I intend on doing so."

Ultimately I spent most of my free time for a year investing personal resources and financial risk to get the camp moving. I would make a call to someone I thought could help, and they would advise me to call someone else to cover other aspects of logistics and so forth. The Holy Spirit took me step by step because I had no idea what I was doing. I was a man on a mission and I would not take 'no' for an answer. After some time, my father began to hear the call also. He was being called by God to support the mission of the camp. He took the step of faith and proceeded to give many hours of his time to support this project. Eventually the pieces of Camp Veritas fell into place and the Camp was ready to receive camper enrollments.

I have generally been successful in my worldly endeavors throughout my whole life. I have always done well in school, work, finances and so forth. I 'succeeded' at most things I attempted. With regards to the camp, the number of enrollments compared to my expectations was pathetic. We were not even close to reaching the minimum number of campers that we had negotiated in our contract with the secular camp we planned to rent for the week. I felt like the Ark had been built, it was raining heavily, but nobody was getting into the boat. Frankly, it was a really distressing time.

In the worldly sense, I had failed. I had tried my very best and I had failed. I was ready to give up and cancel the project. It was at this moment of decision, lying in bed late one night, that I prayed to God in relative despair. Much to my surprise and relief, thoughts from the Lord suddenly flowed through my mind. He made me aware that it was not *my* money I had spent on camp, nor *my* time. In fact, Camp Veritas was not *my* camp at all. The Lord reminded me that I had already given Him everything that I am. My life is His. It was therefore *His* money, *His* time, *His* camp. **There was also no such thing as failure in attempting to do the will of the Lord because, in obeying Him—in taking those steps up that mountain—I have already won.** God never guaranteed *worldly* success. He did, however, promise to provide me with peace and joy if I obeyed, and ultimately, on that front, He came through.

He then gave me a more dramatic vision. The Camp Veritas paradigm would ultimately exist in every diocese of the country as a "boot camp for souls." Our youth would all attend camp as the norm for their Catholic upbringing in their immediate pre and post Confirmation time. They would take spiritual tools from camp that could be applied in their home, their church, and their community for years to come. They would take the spiritual fire they received from the camp and use it to expel the darkness they encountered in our culture. They would participate in the transfiguration of the "Mystical Body of Christ." They would participate in the revolution against the "religion of individualism."

As I saw this vision in my mind, I literally laughed out loud. I felt like the elderly, childless Sarah when God assured her husband Abraham that "you will have descendants as numerous as the stars."(Gen22:17) I brashly told God that He had better get cracking given that our Camp Veritas pioneer year did not look like it was going to get off the ground. God was silent in the midst of my sarcasm, so I went back to my journey and took another step up the mountain.

After observing my climb up this mountain in the fog, to their credit, my immediate family 'spiritually shrugged their shoulders' and started to climb the same mountain of faith as well. It is through the giving of themselves, their talents, life experiences, ideas, and time that God got the camp moving. Each member of my family is a great spiritual warrior, bringing many souls to our Lord.

Ultimately, God's camp worked out. Over fifty youth attended the first year, supported by more than twenty-five adult volunteers. The spiritual program was led by the renowned Franciscan Friars of the Renewal. Camp Veritas was everything I had hoped for. Every camper that attended indicated on the post-camp questionnaire the desire to return the following year. We were delighted that the kids got so much out of it. On the last day of camp one kid said, "You saved a lot of souls this week, including my own." As a God-given bonus many of my own family members contributed their talents and we grew closer in the Lord as a family unit. In the end, the Camp was a total success by both spiritual and worldly measures. Interestingly God more than doubled the enrollments the second year of camp. We now have faith that each year God will provide us with His "perfect number" of enrollments.

I learned through this experience to be at peace with God's plan and give up control. I learned that the Lord will use me in ways I would not have expected. I learned not to put limits on the Lord and to stop guessing how long and difficult the journey will be up the mountain of my life. I learned to increase my faith and trust in the Lord. I learned how to properly measure success in my life. **I learned that nothing is impossible with God!**

The Camp Veritas portion of my journey up the mountain of life continues for me, my family, the campers, the adult volunteers, the dedicated priests and friars, and the camper's parents. If you have an interest in learning more about the camp—the boot camp for souls—please check us out at www.campveritas.com.

DISCIPLESHIP

W HEN I STARTED TO journey with the Lord up this 'mountain of fog' in faith, I had some fear. One of my greatest fears was that the Lord might call me to be a hermit in Africa. In giving up control of my life to Him, becoming a hermit might actually be a possibility. What I have found is that if I am to truly give up control to Him, another possibility is that the Lord may decide He would like me to be a steward of worldly wealth and may have me become financially "successful." What I am discovering through prayer and experience is that the wealth I have in my soul has very little to do with the monetary wealth I have. That is why one might find as many millionaires who are completely miserable as poor people who are blissfully joyful. In short, money has everything to do with temporal 'happiness' and very little to do with lasting 'joy.'

It reminds me of a scene in a movie called "Ironman"(2008). There is this billionaire character, who is all alone in his life, and who is captured by terrorists and thrown into a prison cell. In the cell with him is a poor gentleman who has a loving family which he longs to rejoin. After sharing their respective stories, the poor man ultimately tells the billionaire, "You have everything, yet you have nothing." How true that statement is for so many people across the financial spectrum.

Now it turns out that when we look at the lives of the saints, some of them were, in fact, financially wealthy kings or popes, yet many were poor like St. Francis. In the end, *the attachment* to worldly goods is

what it is we must avoid. A saint can live the life set forth by God in peace and joy, using the 'stuff' God chooses to give to him or not. The saint must always be ready to give back the Lord's "stuff" to Him when He asks for it. That is the moment of truth experienced by the 'rich man' in Scripture who was unwilling to "sell all he had and follow the Lord." That is why for most, "it is easier for a camel to pass through the eye of a needle than for a rich man to enter the Kingdom of Heaven."(Mt19:24)

With monetary wealth, it is also easy to forget whose 'stuff' it is. Being a god unto oneself and forgetting that "there is a God and I am not Him" is much easier if the person is financially wealthy. It is easier for the wealthy to forget about their dependence on God. Poor people do not have as many of these spiritual problems because all they have is their trust in the Lord.

In trying to discern what God wanted me to do with my life, I needed to first identify who I am. At my Baptism, the Lord bestowed three gifts on me. He made me a priest, prophet, and king. I am a priest because I am called to sanctity, holiness, and prayer. I am a prophet because the Lord will use me through the grace of the Sacraments to bring others to Him. Finally, I am a king. I am heir to the Kingdom of Heaven. I am called to live a life of Christian dignity in Christ.

In my discernment, I had to also identify the vocation the Lord had chosen for me. That vocation could be to remain single, become a priest or religious, or enter into marriage. For many, this question of discernment is very difficult to answer. I prayed hard to give up control to the Lord. In giving up control, this meant I had to give up my attachment to the ideas I had for myself and my life. At the very least, I had to open my heart to all of the possibilities of vocation, including that of the priesthood and single life.

Due to my somewhat dense nature, the Lord's communication with me is usually basic and blunt. He is not normally vague or elusive. I knew within five minutes after meeting my future wife that she was my 'eve.' "Bone of my bone and flesh of my flesh," (Gen2:23) it was like I had truly, finally, come into the presence of the other half of my being. My soul somehow recognized her. I know this type of event isn't common or typical so I can't claim that this is how God speaks to everyone. What I do know is that God will answer the prayer of vocation to all who ask. He will answer this prayer to all who *die to their will* and are willing to open their lives to His control. He will place a burning (or nagging) desire of vocation in those who pray for that.

What the Lord asks of me is that I use the talents and gifts He gave me for *His* glory, not for mine. He built me with the intelligence and personality to work in health care, so I am a Physician Assistant for His glory. He has called me to be a husband and father. I have therefore been married for eleven years and have five children for His glory. He has given me the talent of singing; I therefore cantor at my church. He has given me the ability to speak; I therefore minister to all who are open to hearing the Truth, and many who are not. He has given me the ability to teach; I am therefore writing this book. I must always remind myself that in all that I do, in all that I achieve, I am nothing but dust, as are my 'accomplishments.' The only thing that is eternal is my choice to live for God's glory and not for my own.

God has given each of us a myriad of talents and abilities. He will use us uniquely as we are created uniquely. The "Body of Christ" has many parts. Although the parts are different, they are all special and important. My path up the mountain is likely to be somewhat different than yours because we are different parts of this one, living, organic community. We are uniquely made.

God has built some of us to be professional athletes, so be the best athlete you can be for the glory of God. He has built others to stay at home and raise children; so raise the greatest, holiest children for the glory of God. He has built others to be investment bankers; so be a great banker for the glory of God. God has built others to be garbage collectors; so be the best garbage collector this world has ever seen for His glory. No matter what our talents, we have the chance to stand out as an example to others and give God glory. Wherever this journey with the Lord leads us, we have a chance to be a light in the darkness.

In giving up our lives to Him and allowing Him to be our Master, there is peace and joy in everything we do. Although our lives may seem very 'ordinary' to most, when we are living our lives for the Lord, whether we are teachers or housekeepers or doctors, there is nothing 'ordinary' about our lives. We have purpose. We have reason for our being. We have life. We have freedom.

God has a plan for you. Isn't that a cool thought? God has an adventure in store for you from this point forward, an adventure that will have you climbing higher on the 'mountain of life' than you had ever dreamed possible. He has an adventure planned for you whereby He will expand the capacity of your very being in every aspect of your life. He is calling *you* to shine like the sun. He is ready to tap *your* incredible potential. *You* are called to be the greatest saint this world has ever seen. Walk with the Lord on this journey! Never stray from His side! Never lose hope! Never forget about the finish line!

I pray that the Lord will mold me into His image. I pray for the grace to do His will. I pray that we will all have the courage to reach up and take His hand and allow Him to lead us in this first step up our personal mountain of life to His Glory forever and ever! Amen.

SUMMARY: TIDBITS OF WISDOM

The following lists the phrases that were highlighted in bold print:

- Science is the study of the creation of God.
- If you constantly choose God, you will have peace and joy at all times, in every situation.
- Without God, there is no order. Without God, there is no Truth. Without God, there is no such thing as good and evil.
- The Church is ill because the family is ill.
- The Church is the antithesis of the "religion of individualism."
- With the Holy Spirit, there is no such thing as odds.
- There is a God and I am not Him.
- If our morality and Truth is relative and individual, we cannot believe in God.
- If you really believe in God, you therefore must believe in objective Truth.
- God will always answer your prayer if it is healthy for you.
- If we could die to ourselves, if we could die to our will, we lose all of our fear and become children of God.

- All who want to be God get their own kingdom absent of the true God. We call that Hell.
- Most people in the world are teenagers.
- For those who love the Lord, there is no difference between venial and mortal sins, because in both cases, you are hurting your relationship with the Lord.
- God will take you as you are.
- God has allowed us to have children so we could have an idea about how He feels about us.
- The Last Supper is the Passion.
- There are no accidents.
- Behold, I am the handmaid of the Lord, may it be done to me according to Your word.
- Every human being, regardless of what they have done before, is called to be a saint now.
- Saints are not people who never sin. Saints are people who have fallen to sin but keep getting up.
- Ultimately, every saint has a past and every sinner has a future.
- Has God changed?
- The end does not justify the means.
- Extramarital sex is always an affront to a lasting, healthy, marital relationship.
- "Tolerance" of sin and evil has never been, nor should ever be, a Catholic virtue.
- It is through the apathy about sin by good people that sin has taken a stronghold in today's world.
- We are all hypocrites.
- We must judge actions as good or evil.
- Abortion and Embryonic Stem Cell Research are acts always rooted in selfishness.
- If the Lord loves me, what else really matters?
- There is no such thing as failure in attempting to do the will of the Lord because in obeying Him, I have already won.
- Nothing is impossible with God.
- The attachment to worldly goods is what we must avoid.

Epilogue

JESUS SAYS IN JOHN 14:6,

> "I am the way and the **truth** and the life.
> No one comes to the Father except through me."

Resources

Information about **Camp Veritas**, a Catholic camp for youth, can be found at www.campveritas.com.

If you enjoyed *Climbing Veritas Mountain*, you may want to read *Calling All POWs* by Robert A. Young.

About the Author

Ryan Young is a Physician Assistant who lives and works in New York State. Ryan is the founder of Camp Veritas, an outdoor camp for Catholic youth. He currently serves in a voluntary capacity as the Director of the camp.

Ryan attended the Franciscan University of Steubenville in Steubenville, Ohio, and Saint Francis University in Loretto, Pennsylvania.

Ryan's wife, Elizabeth, is also a Physician Assistant. Ryan and Elizabeth have been blessed with five children: Christopher, Trinity, Grace, Mary, and Justice.